OCCUPATION: DEATH

A TANNER NOVEL - BOOK 12

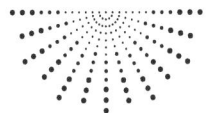

REMINGTON KANE

INTRODUCTION

OCCUPATION: DEATH – A TANNER NOVEL – BOOK 12

With Alonso Alvarado dead and the threat to his friends in New York City eliminated, Tanner returns to doing what he alone does best, as he takes a contract on a man who has proven impossible to kill.

ACKNOWLEDGMENTS

I write for you.

—Remington Kane

1
IT'S TIME TO GO TO WORK

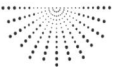

HONOLULU, HAWAII

Tanner and Alexa were staying at a luxury hotel but had spent most of their time either on the beach or off exploring the other islands.

Alexa told Tanner that she was as happy as she had ever been. She also remarked that she had never seen him look so mellow.

They made love often and had done so at sunrise on a deserted stretch of beach. Tanner had seldom spent so much time with one woman, but he found himself wanting more of Alexa each day. A year ago, he would have been guarded with Alexa, as he distrusted the emotion of romantic love. However, admitting his love for Laurel Ivy had made him less wary, because they had been able to stay close and hadn't ended in disaster.

The fact that Laurel married Joe Pullo made him glad, not angry, because he knew himself well enough to know he could never have given Laurel the life she wanted. He liked New York City a great deal, but he wasn't ready to settle down or retire from being an assassin, and he hadn't known anything approaching a normal life since he was a boy of sixteen.

∼

THEY WERE RECLINING IN LOUNGE CHAIRS OUT BY THE pool when Alexa sat up and grabbed her beach robe.

"I'll be right back. I'm out of lotion. If you see a waiter, tell him to bring me another drink."

"Will do," Tanner said.

He was enjoying Hawaii, but Conrad Burke had gotten in touch with him that morning via an email account and Tanner agreed that he would consider taking a contract.

The man who had survived despite the best efforts of the U.S. Government had yet to resurface, but Burke wanted Tanner brought up to speed on the target in case an opportunity arose to take the man out.

Tanner told Burke he would consider accepting the contract once he knew all the facts and Burke said that he would be sending one of his people to see him sometime that day.

Earlier, when Tanner passed through the lobby on the way back to his hotel room, he expected to find a message waiting for him when he checked with the front desk. He was looking forward to finding out who the target was that had proven so difficult to kill, and he was ready to leave paradise and get back to work.

Tanner smiled inwardly. The words, "It's time to go to work," was the code phrase Burke had given him to remember. Burke said that when his employee made contact, that they would use that phrase to identify themselves. Afterwards, Tanner would be given the details of the contract they wanted him to fulfill.

While in the lobby that morning, a man had approached him. Tanner thought that maybe he was Burke's representative coming to make contact, and that he would give him details about the hit they wanted him to perform.

When the man spoke and the first words out of his mouth were, "It's time to go…" Tanner was certain it was Burke's man and that he was uttering the identifying phrase, "It's time to go to work." But no, instead, the man said, "It's time to go to the meeting. Do you know what conference room it's in?"

"I don't know what you're talking about," Tanner told the man.

"The meeting of regional managers for Kirby Vacuums, aren't you the guy that runs the Seattle Division?"

"No," Tanner said.

"Oh," the man said, as he took a pair of thick glasses from his pocket and put them on. When he got a good look at Tanner, he gave him a weak smile. "Sorry, but there was this hot girl at the bar and I took my glasses off when I went to talk to her, you know how it is."

"Goodbye," Tanner said, and the man moved away in a hurry.

AFTER ALEXA LEFT TO GET MORE LOTION, TANNER SHUT his eyes for just a few moments, but when he sensed movement, he opened them and saw a woman taking Alexa's place beside him, as the beauty stretched out atop a chaise lounge.

It was Sara Blake, the same woman who had seen to Dan Matthews' torture and interrogation weeks earlier, although Tanner had no knowledge of her involvement.

Sara looked sexy with her long raven hair shining and blue eyes sparkling with mischief. The red bikini she wore was not only small, but daringly so, and she had the body for it.

She smiled at Tanner. "Aren't you going to say hello?"

"I'm hoping it's a bad dream and I'll wake up soon."

Sara laughed. "I'm real, and I think it's plain to see that I'm not concealing any weapons."

Tanner took off his sunglasses and gave her a long measuring look.

"What are you doing here, Blake?"

Sara's smile widened.

"It's time to go to work."

2

NORMAL

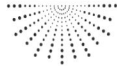

At poolside in Honolulu, Hawaii, Tanner looked over at Sara Blake, who was wearing a revealing red bikini, and asked her a question.

"Would you say that again?"

"I said, 'It's time to go to work.'"

"Work?"

"I believe Mr. Burke explained that he wanted to use your services, although he never went into details. I'm here to give you those details."

Tanner sat up and swung his legs around until his feet touched the floor.

"Both Matthews and Burke said that I had a fan in his organization, that was you?"

"It was me. By the way, Dan Matthews has been handled. I took care of it myself in Panama."

"Took care of it how, is he dead?"

"No, that's your specialty, although he was tortured, and I hear there's a possibility that he'll be imprisoned for espionage soon."

"Why are you working for Burke?"

"If you'll remember, Mr. Burke gave Jenny, Jake, and myself a ride home on his jet. It was a long flight and Mr. Burke and I talked on the plane. He wanted fresh blood in his company and I needed a new start. I went to work for Conrad Burke shortly after we returned from Guambi, and when the U.S. Government came to the Burke corporation wanting to outsource assassinations, you naturally came to mind."

"And what's your part in all this?"

"I'll be acting as a liaison between you and the Burke corporation. Once you agree to take a contract, it will be up to me to see that you get all the help you need, including materials, travel arrangements, and logistics."

Tanner seldom displayed surprise or amazement, but both those emotions were appearing on his face as he processed Sara's words.

"*You* want to help me carry out contracts? *You?*"

Sara laughed and then stretched out on the chaise lounge with her arms above her head.

"I'm not the same woman you knew in New York."

Tanner heard her words, but his eyes were busy taking in her body. He didn't know how long she'd been in Honolulu, but she was tanned, and damned delectable. His eyes were taking in the swell of her breasts, which were practically spilling out of her bikini top, when Alexa's voice made him jerk his head up.

"I see you found a way to amuse yourself while I was gone."

Tanner stood. "Alexa, this is Sara Blake. She's a…"

Sara stood as well, and offered Alexa her hand, as she smiled at Tanner.

"Tanner and I are old friends."

"I see," Alexa said, as she released Sara's hand. "But why are you here?"

"I work for Conrad Burke. Mr. Burke wants to contract with Tanner for a certain service."

"A hit?" Alexa said.

Sara looked at Tanner with surprise showing on her face. "She's aware of your profession?"

"Yes, Blake, Alexa and I both took down Alvarado in Mexico."

"Ah, she's that woman, and the two of you are still together, interesting."

Alexa crossed her arms over her chest. "Why is that interesting to you?"

"It's just that I assumed you had met here and were just involved in a little… playtime. Tanner doesn't seem the type to have a long-term relationship."

"Blake, get to the point of your visit," Tanner said.

"All right, Mr. Burke would like to know when you'll be ready to work."

"We were planning to leave Hawaii in two days," Tanner said. "You can tell Burke that I'll be available after that, but I'll want details before I agree to anything."

"That's fine. I'll leave a package for you at the front desk that will contain an encrypted cell phone. When you're ready to talk, just call the number in the phone's directory."

"Who will answer?" Tanner asked.

"I will. But tell me, when you leave here, will you be headed back to New York City?"

"No, we were thinking of going to L.A."

"That's good; New York holds too many bad memories for me."

Tanner saw that Alexa's hands were empty. "I thought you went off to buy more sun blocker?"

"When I was halfway there my little voice told me to return to you. Now I know why."

Sara looked back and forth at them. "Little voice?"

"Alexa is psychic."

Sara grinned. "Really?"

"Yes, really," Alexa said, with a sneer in her voice.

Sara offered Tanner her hand. He took it and found that she had a firm grip.

"I'll expect that call, and it was good to meet you, Alexa."

Sara walked off, and both Tanner and Alexa watched her until she disappeared back into the hotel.

"She's very beautiful, were you two ever lovers?"

"No."

"Really? Because I sensed very strong emotions between the two of you."

Tanner smiled bitterly. "It's a long story. Let's go into the bar and I'll tell it to you."

AT A CORNER TABLE INSIDE THE HOTEL BAR, ALEXA LEANED back in her seat and blew out a sigh.

"That's quite a story, Tanner. Are you sure you can trust this Sara?"

"Despite everything that's happened between us in the past, yes. I trust her to a degree. Which means, I don't think she still wants to kill me."

Alexa made a face. "Her emotions may have swung the other way, or why else show up dressed in a bikini?"

"This is a vacation resort and we were at a pool, so why not? Believe me, Alexa, Sara Blake may not want me dead any longer, but she's also not looking to hook up with me."

"I'm not so sure, but let me ask you a question. What are your feelings for her?"

"I used to feel annoyance and pity for her, but I'm glad

to see that she's starting over. Burke likely gave her this assignment because he knows the two of us worked together in Guambi to save Sara's sister."

"Maybe she wasn't assigned; she might have asked to work with you."

"Maybe, and as much as she once hated me, she never doubted my skills. She knows I'll be successful if I decide to take the contract. That success may help her rise in Burke's organization."

"Will you take the contract?"

"That depends on the details."

Alexa grew quiet and looked out at the ocean through the enormous picture window that made up the left side of the bar. When she had finished thinking about the situation, she reached across and took Tanner's hand.

"Call this Sara Blake and invite her to dinner. I want to get to know her better, and perhaps we'll learn more about the contract."

"You mean tonight?"

"Yes, the more we know and the sooner we know it, the better I'll feel."

Tanner gave Alexa's hand a squeeze. "Don't worry. Blake isn't a threat. If she still wanted to hurt me, there would be no way for her to hide her feelings. She's a woman of strong passion."

Alexa smiled bitterly. "You said that she was once full of hate; that sort of emotion doesn't just disappear."

Tanner took out the encrypted phone Sara had left for him. He had retrieved it from the front desk before entering the bar.

Sara answered on the fourth ring, and she knew it was him.

"Hello, Tanner."

"Let me guess, I'm the only one you gave this number to?"

"Yes, both your phone and mine are strictly for work."

"Alexa and I want to take you to dinner tonight, Blake. We're both curious about what Burke wants me to do."

"Dinner sounds good, but it will be on me; after all, I'm the one with the expense account."

"Fine, any preference?"

"There's a steakhouse just off the lobby; will that do?"

"That's good for us, what time?"

"I'll call and make a reservation for eight o'clock."

"We'll see you then," Tanner said, and he ended the call.

"How did she sound?" Alexa asked.

"Normal."

"There's nothing normal about her. She's here to ask you to kill someone."

Tanner smiled. "For me, that's normal."

3
SOLO ASSASSIN

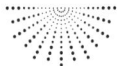

THE STEAKHOUSE SERVED EXCELLENT FOOD ON LINEN tablecloths, while the silverware was heavy, and the lighting muted.

Tanner and Alexa had arrived on time to find that Sara was already waiting for them. Sara was wearing a simple black dress with a short hemline that also revealed a hint of cleavage. Alexa was dressed much the same, only her dress was blue, while Tanner wore gray slacks with a black polo shirt.

They kept the conversation light at first while discussing their impressions of the hotel and the island, but once their appetizers arrived along with their second drinks, the talk turned to business.

"Tell me about the target," Tanner said to Sara. He was seated directly across from her at their round table while Alexa sat on his right and between them.

"His name is Julien Adams. Have you ever heard of him?" Sara asked.

"No, why, is he famous?"

"Not famous, but he is known in financial circles. Julien Adams is fifty-two, never married, no children. When he was twenty-eight he inherited real estate holdings worth seventeen million dollars. Adams quadrupled that fortune inside ten years and then turned his attention toward the stock market. After ten more years had passed, the man was worth half a billion."

"Matthews said that the target was involved with terrorists, is that true?"

"Yes, but the government believes that Adams is funding terrorists as a means to increase his personal fortune. With advance notice of who will be attacked and what will be destroyed, Adams is able to short stocks in certain industries and profit by their declines after an attack. As far as they know, he's never profited from an attack that's taken place on American soil, but he's made millions by shorting overseas stocks in foreign markets."

Alexa interrupted. "I've heard the term 'shorting a stock' for years, but I don't know what it means."

Tanner attempted to enlighten her. "Let's say that you believe that the stock of ABC Corporation will lose value in the future. You would call your broker and ask him to find 100 shares of ABC Corporation that you can borrow for a short sale. The current price of ABC Corporation is $50 a share. That would make your 100 borrowed shares worth $5,000, right?"

Alexa nodded. "I'm with you so far."

"Now remember, your account is being credited with that $5,000, although you haven't paid for the stock. So, a week later, the price has dropped, and shares of ABC Corporation now trade for $40 a share. You now pay back the 100 borrowed shares, which covers your short position, for $40 each, spending $4,000, and your profit on the trade is $1,000, which is the difference between the beginning value of the 100 shares at $50, and the value of the shares when you paid back the 100 shares at $40 a share. Get it?"

Alexa smiled. "I'm more confused than ever."

"Talk to a stockbroker," Tanner said, as he returned her smile.

Sara cleared her throat and continued. "Anyway, the government has been unable to prove that Adams is funding terrorists to have information on future attacks, but there's evidence from four separate sources that point to Adams as profiting by acts of terrorism."

"Wouldn't doing this leave a trace behind in his portfolio transactions?" Tanner asked.

"Yes, but Adams is too smart to make the moves himself, and the government has four witnesses that say they were used by Adams as front men. They gave him up as a way of avoiding their own legal troubles."

"All right, so why has this man proven to be so difficult to kill?"

"For starters, he's incredibly hard to locate. He owns dozens of properties and has access to many more through a network of equally rich business associates. All of these homes are in secluded locations and Adams surrounds himself with security."

"Then I'll have to find him first. That shouldn't be difficult if you can point me toward someone who knows him well."

Sara stared at Tanner for a moment before continuing. "You should know that three men have already died while trying to kill Adams. Two of them are presumed dead, while the third man, an ex-Navy SEAL named Cameron Bonds was later found on a beach in Barcelona. Bonds' body had been ravaged by its time in the water, but the cause of death was drowning."

"Did the body have any ligature marks on it?" Tanner

asked.

"No, nor were there any other signs of a major trauma. Cameron Bonds simply drowned. It's being theorized that he was just left abandoned in the middle of the Mediterranean Sea. If the same sort of thing was done to the other men, then it's no wonder that their bodies haven't been found."

Their steaks arrived, and they ate while talking little. Tanner noticed that Alexa and Sara kept eyeing each other during the meal.

Tanner knew that Alexa didn't like Sara but had no idea how Sara felt about Alexa. He supposed she might be annoyed by her presence during the talk about the contract and target, but Tanner trusted Alexa and Sara would have to do so as well.

When all three of them finished their meals, Sara gave Tanner a bit of mystifying news.

"The former Navy SEAL whose body was recovered, Cameron Bonds, he was in contact with a mole inside Adams' organization. In their last communication, Bonds stated that he had killed Adams by blowing the man's head off. Since that time, the mole has seen Adams from a distance and stated that Adams is healthy and shows no signs of injury."

"Curious," Tanner said. "And I doubt an ex-Navy SEAL would lie about completing a mission."

"No, he wouldn't, and so it's been theorized that Bonds was forced to lie about killing Adams for some purpose, but what that purpose was, no one knows."

"Perhaps Adams found out he had a spy in his organization and was trying to make the mole reveal himself," Alexa said.

"That is one theory," Sara agreed. "If so, it failed.

Bonds only had a way to pass messages back and forth. He never knew the mole's identity."

The women indulged in dessert while Tanner only had coffee. Once she finished eating her chocolate mousse, Sara wiped her mouth and asked Tanner if he was taking the contract.

"Yes, because it sounds like a challenge, and also because Adams is the worst sort of dirtbag, the type that profits off other people's misery."

Sara smiled at his answer. "Excellent, and our first stop after leaving Hawaii is to fly to Burke's US corporate headquarters in Connecticut. They'll have the latest Intel waiting for us and Mr. Burke will also be there, as well as your back-up support."

"I work alone, Blake, you know that."

Sara gestured at Alexa. "If you work alone, then why is she here, and why was she in Mexico with you?"

"Alexa and I had a mutual desire to see Alvarado dead, but I'm a solo assassin and I won't be burdened with one of Burke's flunkies."

"The man isn't a flunky, he's an arms specialist. I asked Mr. Burke to assign him to you so that you would be equipped with the best."

Tanner nodded. "That could be a good thing, if the man knows his stuff."

"I've been assured that he does, however, there is one more thing."

"Here it comes," Alexa said.

"What do you mean by that?" Sara asked her.

"I mean that I don't trust you. Not after Tanner told me about your past actions. I've been expecting you to drop something nasty on us ever since I learned about you."

"You know nothing about me," Sara said, and then she

turned back to Tanner. "I've voiced my disagreement with the decision, but there is someone at the Burke Corporation who wants you to give a demonstration before we finalize our arrangement."

"Who is this someone?"

"He's Burke Corporation CFO Sloane Lennox. The demonstration consists of making it through a gauntlet run by his personal bodyguard, a man named Brad Grant, and some of Burke's elite security personnel. It's not targeted at you, Lennox even put the ex-Navy SEALs through this stupid test."

"I won't do it," Tanner said.

Disappointment filled Sara's face as she let out a sigh. "You're not taking the contract?"

"No, I've already said I'll kill Julien Adams, but I won't take a test. I'm not a job applicant, I'm the best killer in the world and I don't need to prove that to anyone."

Sara smiled. "You are the most confident man I know."

"You admire him?" Alexa asked.

Sara ignored her and spoke to Tanner. "I'll send pictures of Julien Adams to your phone soon, along with details about our departure from the island. We'll all be flying together on one of Mr. Burke's jets. Do you have any other questions?"

"No."

Sara gave a curt nod. "Good."

After paying the bill, Sara left the table first, as Tanner and Alexa watched her walk away.

"Be careful around that bitch, Tanner."

"Of course I will, but I don't believe she wants me dead."

Alexa turned back around and looked at him. "Maybe she just wants you."

"No, Alexa, Blake would sleep with the devil before she'd ever touch me."

"Maybe," Alexa said, "Or maybe not."

4
THERE'S NO SUCH THING AS NOTHING

After Alexa fell asleep on the plane ride to Connecticut, Tanner got up to use the restroom.

As he was walking back to his seat, Sara asked him to sit beside her.

Tanner did so, and Sara held up her phone to reveal a new photo of Julien Adams. Adams was blond, with pale skin, of average height, and had full lips. His eyes were brown, but looked hooded, as if he were always on the verge of falling asleep.

"Where was this taken?" Tanner asked.

"In Madrid, two weeks ago. An Australian tourist posted his vacation photos on Facebook when he returned home and Adams was in the background of one of the photos."

"The government's facial recognition software discovered this?"

"Yes."

Tanner grimaced. "I hope I stay off their radar. Technology is making it harder and harder to evade the authorities."

"I know that photo is two weeks old, but maybe Adams is still in Spain."

"Maybe, but I'll need to verify his current location."

"How do you plan to do that?"

"I'll ask Adams' suspected terrorist contact, Omar Ali Rashid. Rashid's current location is known."

"Rashid has never been officially tied to terrorists, however, the evidence is overwhelming that he is sympathetic to certain extreme organizations. If the man's brother wasn't a diplomat, I doubt he would be allowed in the country."

"He may wish to leave when I get done with him."

"If you kill him that could lead to problems."

"I won't kill him, if that file you gave me concerning him is accurate, I won't have to."

"All right, but won't he simply call Adams and warn him once you've talked to him?"

Tanner smiled. "Leave that to me."

They sat quietly together for a moment, but then Sara spoke.

"I'm sorry you lost Sophia."

"Thank you."

"I also read in the paper that Laurel and Joe married."

"Yes."

"I'm sorry, Tanner. That must have hurt, even if you and Joe are friends."

"It was the best thing all around."

"Because you're not the marrying type?"

"I suppose not."

"Does Alexa know that?"

Tanner turned in his seat and stared at Sara. "What's your deal, Blake?"

"What do you mean?"

"I mean why are you here? About a year ago, you were

a federal agent hunting me down for revenge and now you're trying to help me. It doesn't compute."

Sara gave a slight shrug. "I've changed. And despite the fact that you killed Brian, you also saved my sister's life. If you hadn't gone to Guambi with me... well, I think I'd be dead as well. Jake Garner also owes you his life."

"That may all be true, but it's still unusual for someone to change so much in so short a period."

"It's also unusual for a woman to lose two lovers in a matter of months, but I've done that as well."

Tanner straightened in his seat as he asked Sara a question. "How is your sister doing?"

"She's great, and she and Jake are engaged. The wedding will take place this summer."

Tanner smiled. "I assume I'm not invited."

"Tanner, if it weren't for the fact that so many Feds would be attending, I think you would get an invitation. I also know what you did for Jake, by handing him that Chemzonic bust in Oklahoma City. That was huge, Tanner, and Jake's already been promoted."

"It's nice to know that if the feds ever form a task force against me, that someone I know might be running it."

"I don't think you have to worry about Jake coming after you."

"And what about you, Blake? I really hope this isn't some elaborate scheme to try to kill me."

Sara looked offended, and then she gripped Tanner's hand and gave it a squeeze.

"I have no hate in my heart for you anymore," Sara said.

Tanner looked down at her hand, and Sara removed it.

"Maybe it's you who hates me. If so, I could understand it. I did try to kill you."

"I don't hate you, Blake."

"Why?" Sara said.

"Why don't I hate you?"

"No, why am I still alive after trying to kill you? Is it that you're honoring the deal we made back in New York City… or is it something else?"

"It's like you said, Blake, we made a deal."

Tanner rose from his seat. When he looked back at Sara, he saw that she was smiling.

"What's that smile about?"

"You insist on calling me Blake although I've told you to call me Sara, why?"

"It keeps things on a professional level, and since all we ever personally felt for each other is animosity, keeping things professional is a good thing, no?"

"I suppose, and anyway, I don't even know your first name."

"That's because you don't need to."

Sara looked in Alexa's direction. "She knows your real name though, doesn't she?'

"Yes."

"Interesting."

Tanner said nothing more and returned to his seat, where he was surprised to see that Alexa was awake, although her head was still resting on a pillow.

"I overheard most of your conversation," Alexa said.

"And?"

"And I want you to think about something."

"What's that?"

"Sara claims that she no longer hates you, well then, what does she feel for you?"

"Nothing, she feels nothing for me."

"Nature abhors a vacuum, Tanner, remember that."

Tanner grew quiet, as he thought about Alexa's words.

5

PAINT AIN'T COOL

AT THE HEADQUARTERS OF THE BURKE CORPORATION IN Connecticut, Sara attempted to persuade Burke CFO Sloane Lennox out of insisting that Tanner be tested. She was in Conrad Burke's office along with Burke, Lennox, and Lennox's bodyguard, a man named Brad Grant.

Sloane Lennox had been with the Burke Corporation since graduating from Yale at twenty-one. He was now in his fifties, the father of two grown children and quite influential inside the Burke Corporation. Lennox was also a quintessential wasp and a pain in the ass.

He had been a boyhood friend of Frank Richards, the late CEO of MegaZenith, who was also the corporate leader of the Conglomerate. Lennox was Richards' best man when Richards was wed. However, Lennox had no inkling of Richards' dark side or nefarious activities and would have been aghast had he known how hungry for power his friend had become.

A loyal employee, as well as a friend, Lennox would do whatever Conrad Burke asked of him, but he found

Burke's expansion into outsourcing assassinations for the US Government to be unwise and distasteful.

He understood that there were people in the world that needed slaying for the greater good of all, such as brutal dictators and terrorists. Nonetheless, he didn't think they should be handled by multi-national corporations.

Still, the government's trained assassins were one thing. Tanner was another matter altogether, and Lennox thought of him as little better than the men who would be targeted. Tanner was a hit man, not a well-trained and battle-tested soldier. And to pay the man a million dollars, well, in Lennox's opinion, that was just insane.

"The ex-Navy SEALs all took the test; why can't this man Tanner do the same?" Lennox asked Sara.

"Tanner is not like other men," Sara said.

"Bullshit!" said Brad Grant. He was six-foot-six and looked like an action figure come to life. He was muscular, handsome, and had perfect teeth. He was also as arrogant as Lennox was, although the trait in Grant sprang from his physical stature and not from a sense of entitlement, as was the case with Lennox.

Brad Grant had hit on Sara more than once in the short time she'd been with the company. He thought of her as a cold bitch because she showed no interest in him. And yet, he still looked Sara over with a lustful gaze every time they crossed paths.

"Tanner is nothing but a lowlife criminal," Grant said. "He's probably afraid to be shown up for the lucky bastard he is."

"Why do you say he's lucky?" Sara asked.

"The guy killed Alonso Alvarado even though Alvarado was being guarded inside a fortress and had hundreds of armed men protecting him. No one, but no one is good enough to overcome those odds, therefore he had to be lucky."

Sara laughed. "If luck is his secret than he's the luckiest man who ever lived. But it's not luck, it's skill. Tanner is as skilled an assassin as has ever lived. He's taken the contract. That means that he'll kill Julien Adams. Let the man be and he'll get to work."

Sloane Lennox shook his head. "We're paying the man the insane amount of a million dollars. He can jump through a few hoops, Miss Blake."

Sara walked over to where Conrad Burke sat behind his desk. The desk was an antique, and had been used by Burke's grandfather, who had founded the company at sixteen. The multi-billion-dollar Burke Corporation began as a general store over a hundred years earlier.

"You've met Tanner. He won't put up with this nonsense."

"Nonsense?" Lennox said, but he grew quiet when Burke raised his hand.

Burke stood and walked around the desk to stand beside Sara. "Miss Blake, we will go through with the demonstration. I'm curious to see what Tanner's reaction will be."

Sara smirked. "You must have poked beehives with a stick when you were a boy."

"How did you guess?" Burke said with a smile. He then led the way out of the office.

THE DEMONSTRATION WAS TO BE HELD AT THE REAR OF THE corporation's property, which was bordered by acres of trees. The Burke Corporate Headquarters was designated as a business campus and held numerous buildings that sprawled over hundreds of acres.

There was an obstacle course on a section of land some distance from the main building, where the test was to be held. There was also a small warehouse that had been converted into a private gym for the Burke Security Department. Although Brad Grant was Sloane Lennox's private bodyguard, he was also a member of the Burke worldwide security force and ranked high in its command structure.

Another man was present to observe the test. His name was Deke Mercer. Mercer was a former Marine who was a gifted gunsmith. Deke was in his thirties, built solid, and was handsome, with short cropped dark hair. He was there to meet Tanner, whom he was to work with and assist with weapons.

Sara had been looking at the other security guards and had taken note that they were all huge men. They were dressed in black and carrying paint guns that looked as deadly as the real thing.

Burke's security force had an elite division of men that worked around the world wherever Burke needed more manpower to protect his interests. The men were all highly trained, but few of them were former military.

The guards had all moved up within the ranks and considered themselves to be as good as any soldier, something that a Marine like Deke Mercer scoffed at. Deke had only been at Burke for a short time and had already had an altercation with Brad Grant, after Grant tried to bully him.

Tanner's test would be to survive a paintball contest against ten of Burke's best security personnel without being marked by paint. The other men who had been subjected to the test had faced only three men.

Burke noted the disparity. "Why are there so many men here for the test, Sloane?" Burke asked.

"This criminal, this Tanner, he's supposed to be the best assassin in the world, correct?"

"Yes," Burke said.

"Well then, surviving our little contest should be a thing of ease for him. However, if he fails, then we choose someone else to fulfill the contract. Someone like that Sicilian fellow Brad mentioned."

Lennox's mention of bringing in another hit man caught Sara's attention. "What's this about bringing in a Sicilian, what Sicilian?"

"Maurice Scallato, in Europe, he's known as Il Fantasma, The Ghost," Brad Grant said. "He's an eighth or ninth generation assassin and a legend in Europe. They say he's even better than Lars Gruber was."

"Tanner killed Gruber, so it's obvious that Tanner was also better than Gruber, but never mind that. Tanner has already agreed to take the contract. You can consider Julien Adams dead."

"No money has changed hands yet, young lady," Lennox said, and Tanner won't see a penny until I approve it."

"Then I suggest you approve it," said a voice from behind Lennox, and everyone turned to see Tanner and Alexa walking out of the woods.

Most of the men present stared at Tanner, to take in his measure, while only noticing Alexa. That was true for everyone but Deke Mercer, whose eyes flowed over Alexa with an admiring gaze. When Alexa locked eyes with him, Deke sent her a smile. Alexa didn't smile in return, but she did acknowledge Mercer with a slight nod.

Burke looked surprised by Tanner's sudden appearance and pointed back toward the company campus.

"I sent a golf cart to bring you here."

"We walked, and I'll tell you right now that you can shove this test where the sun don't shine. Pay me and I'll kill Julien Adams. Refuse to pay me and I'll leave now, but I won't play the trained monkey like these rent-a-cops you have here."

Brad Grant moved close to Tanner. The man was several inches taller and outweighed Tanner by fifty pounds of pure muscle. He looked Tanner over and made a sound of distaste.

"Listen, little man, we're not trained monkeys. We're an elite group of security personnel. I think you won't take the test because you know that you'll fail."

"Kick his ass, Brad!" one of the men shouted, he was a young man named Nick Canto who was even larger than Brad Grant. Canto caressed the paint gun he held as if it were a lover, while glaring at Tanner with disdain in his eyes.

Sara placed a hand on Burke's arm. "You need to end this demonstration now before someone gets hurt. Tanner won't play with these idiots—he'll kill them."

Burke read Sara's face and saw the concern in her eyes. He raised up a hand and spoke. "All right. That's enough. The demonstration has been cancelled. Grant, have the men return to the campus."

Lennox scowled. "Conrad, I thought that we had an agreement."

"I changed my mind. Release Tanner's payment, then we can get down to business. This project has had enough delays already."

Brad Grant leaned closer to Tanner. "This is your lucky day, Tanner, but then, you have a lot of lucky days, don't you?"

Tanner said nothing, and Grant turned to walk away.

The punk named Nick Canto, who had mouthed off before, leveled his paint gun at Tanner and fired. The red paint missed Tanner completely, but struck Alexa on the left arm, causing her to hiss in pain while ruining her dress.

Tanner removed a small gun from its pocket holster, took aim, and placed a bullet in the center of Canto's forehead.

6
NO JOKE

"Oh, my, God!" Sloane Lennox cried out, while staring over at the dead security guard named Nick Canto. Canto had fired a paintball at Tanner and hit Alexa in the arm.

Tanner, a man who didn't suffer fools, gladly or otherwise, killed Canto with a shot to the head.

With the fool dead, Tanner turned to Alexa and asked her if she was all right.

"It stings like hell, but there's no damage."

Brad Grant, Canto's supervisor, stared down at the body of the young man and then back at Tanner.

"What the fuck, Tanner! It was just a paintball."

Tanner stared back at him, then he looked at the other eight men holding paintball guns.

"We were here for a demonstration, correct? Does anyone else want me to demonstrate what I do?"

The men all dropped their paintball guns and began moving back toward the golf carts they had rode in on from the main building.

Grant held on to his paintball gun, but he kept the faux weapon pointed at the ground.

Burke stepped forward while rubbing a hand over his face and spoke to Tanner. Burke had been standing behind his two personal bodyguards, who had moved in front of him when Tanner killed Canto. The men had their guns drawn but had put them away when Burke told them to holster their weapons.

"Was it really necessary to kill that man, Tanner?"

"I'm not in the second chance business, Burke. If I detect a threat, I end it." Tanner turned his gaze on Sara. "I made the mistake of giving someone a second chance once before and it nearly cost me my life. That won't happen again."

Sara met Tanner's gaze and gave a little shake of her head. There was anger in Tanner's eyes, along with mistrust. She was afraid that he was blaming her for what had occurred.

Burke saw that Tanner was staring at Sara and he raised a hand. "Miss Blake advised against this several times. I should have listened to her."

Deke Mercer had walked over to Alexa and handed her the shop rag that was perpetually in his rear pocket.

"This rag has a little gun oil on it, but it should help you clean off some of the paint."

Alexa looked up into Deke's blue eyes and smiled. "Thank you, that's very kind."

"Who are you?" Tanner asked Deke.

"The name is Deke Mercer, Tanner. I'm the gunsmith that will be helping you."

Tanner studied Mercer and saw that there was a Marine Corps tattoo on the biceps of one of his muscular arms, while the man had the carriage of someone who knew how to handle himself. Mercer's voice carried with it a Midwest accent.

"Were you part of this test?"

"Hell no, and you can kill as many as these wannabe soldiers as you want. You'll be doing the world a favor."

Brad Grant rushed over and yelled at Deke. "Call me a wannabe soldier to my face, jarhead."

Deke laughed. "We had this conversation once already, didn't we? As I recall, it ended with you spending the night in the hospital."

"You were just lucky," Grant said.

"Grant, leave Deke alone before he gets lucky again," Burke said.

Grant moved away and stood by Lennox's side. Lennox was staring at Tanner as if he were something alien.

"He just killed the man, as if he were simply swatting a fly… and all over a little paint."

Those words were mumbled by Lennox but heard by everyone. Tanner spoke to him.

"Who are you?"

The answer to that question stirred Lennox out of his shock. He straightened his back and answered.

"My name is Sloane Lennox. I'm the Chief Financial Officer for the Burke Corporation."

"You write the checks, good, then pay me and we can get started on killing Julien Adams."

Lennox pointed at the body of Nick Canto. "You have to answer for killing that man."

"Mr. Canto died in a training accident, Sloane," Burke said, "Or so the police will be told."

"Accident? This hoodlum shot the young man in cold blood."

Tanner took a step toward Lennox and the CFO hid behind Brad Grant.

"Keep him away from me."

"Relax, Lennox, I only kill people who are a threat. That leaves you out," Tanner said.

∼

THE POLICE HAD BEEN CALLED AND SEEMED SATISFIED THAT Canto had died in a firearms accident. One of the other security guards took responsibility for the mishap and would deal with the consequences. For doing so, the man would be promoted and given a company car.

Sara had offered Alexa a change of clothes. It was just a jogging outfit that she kept in her office, but the outfit was clean. Alexa declined her offer and opted to keep wearing the dress. The garment was a total loss and Burke told her to send him the bill for its replacement.

Tanner was in Burke's office with Alexa, Sara, Burke, and Deke Mercer. Once the aftermath of the shooting had been settled, Tanner was ready to get to work.

"Do you have any more bullshit you'd like to do, Burke, or can we get down to business?"

"Check your account, Tanner; you'll find that you've been paid."

"Fine, but before I can kill Adams I have to locate him, and to do that, I'll need to make his contact Omar Ali Rashid talk."

"Rashid is in Boston," Sara said.

"I'll fly there as soon as I can get a flight."

"There's a jet at your disposal," Burke said.

"Even better," Tanner said. "We'll leave in two hours; Alexa has to change."

Sara stood. "I'll be accompanying you."

"Why?"

"It's my job, Tanner. If you need anything while we're in Boston, just call me."

Alexa took Tanner's hand. "He won't need anything from you."

Sara sighed softly. "I meant in a professional sense."

"In any sense," Alexa said.

Burke watched this exchange with a worried expression. "Is there a problem, Miss Blake?"

"No sir, just a small clash of personalities. It will work itself out."

Burke caught Tanner's eye. "Would you like someone else assigned to help you, Tanner?"

Tanner stared at Sara before answering. "Blake and I have a history, and better the devil I know than one that I don't know."

"Yes, you two worked well together in Guambi; I hope that continues here."

"We'll see," Tanner said.

Sara stared back at him with an enigmatic smile.

7

A FRESH START

To save time, Alexa returned to their hotel to change clothes and pack while Tanner received a briefing from Sara.

The two of them were alone in a conference room where Sara brought Tanner up to speed on the latest Intel concerning Omar Ali Rashid, whom Tanner would interrogate to learn the whereabouts of Julien Adams.

Sara and Tanner were seated on opposite sides of a large conference table and facing a huge video screen, which was mounted on the wall. Sara pushed a button on a remote control and gave Tanner a slideshow presentation of the condo apartment house where Rashid lived.

"He's guarded by two men at all times and travels in a limo. Nothing major has changed in the man's life since the last information I gave you concerning him. However, as you can see, I arranged to have more pictures of the underground parking garage taken, and from different angles."

"Why did you do that?"

Sara blinked in a show of surprise at Tanner's question

before answering it. "Looking over the data, I thought that the underground garage would be the best place to grab the man. If I was mistaken, I can arrange to have any other areas photographed in detail before we land in Boston."

"No, your assumption was correct. I'll be taking Rashid in the garage."

"What sort of vehicle will you need?"

"I'll steal a van when I get there."

"I thought so, and I arranged to have one waiting for our arrival. It's white, with clean plates. There are also restraints attached to the wall."

"It sounds like the van you once had me in."

Sara stood and moved around the table to take a seat beside Tanner. "I'm not out to hurt you, Tanner. I'm here to help. That's my job now and I plan to do it well."

Tanner locked eyes with her. When Sara met his gaze without flinching, he nodded.

"Fair enough. We'll call this a fresh start. Is there anything else you need to tell me about Rashid?"

"Yes. That underground parking garage has several cameras. If needed, I can arrange to have them disabled before you arrive."

"That won't be necessary. I'll handle it."

"Okay, but I have a request. Don't kill Rashid's guards. That would escalate things in the diplomatic arena where Rashid's brother operates. The men guarding Rashid aren't simply thugs, but former soldiers."

"That won't be a problem either, but now I have a question for you."

"Yes?"

"Deke Mercer, what's his story?"

"As I understand it, Mercer is an ex-Marine and a gifted gunsmith. He was recommended by our government contact and was excited to hear that he'd be working with you."

"Why?"

Sara smiled. "He said that you would probably give him a chance to stretch his skills, and in fact, he would like to see you before we leave for Boston."

Tanner stood. "Why don't we see him now?"

∼

As they were leaving the conference room, Conrad Burke approached them, while walking with his bodyguards, who eyed Tanner carefully. Burke told the men to stay back a few feet before joining Tanner and Sara.

"Tanner, there was something I forgot to inform you about. It's probably nothing, but Brad Grant mentioning the man earlier brought it to mind."

"What man?" Tanner asked.

"A Sicilian assassin named Maurice Scallato, the first time I heard that name was from my ex-brother-in-law, Robert Martinez."

Tanner knew Martinez, the man had been an ally and advisor to Alonso Alvarado.

"What does Martinez have to do with Scallato?"

"Nothing really, but Alvarado had asked Robert to try to contact him. Alvarado wanted to use Scallato as a sort of dead man's switch. From what Robert said, Alvarado wanted to hire Scallato to kill you, but only in the event that you first killed Alvarado. It was to be Alvarado's way of getting revenge from the grave; however, Robert said that Scallato never contacted Alvarado, and thus no money changed hands."

"What about Grant, is he in contact with Scallato?"

Sara made a sound of derision. "Brad Grant probably read about Scallato in one of those soldiers of fortune and mercenary magazines he's always quoting from. It's just talk."

"Thanks for the info, Burke, although I doubt that anything will come of it."

"Neither do I, but I've learned it's better to have as much knowledge about a possible threat as you can. Besides, I wouldn't want you killed before you earn your money."

Burke excused himself as Sara's phone rang, and she was informed that Alexa had returned from her trip to the hotel.

∽

AFTER GREETING ALEXA WITH A KISS IN THE LOBBY, Tanner commented on how quickly her trip back to the hotel went.

"I was taken to and from inside a Burke company van and the driver helped with the luggage."

Tanner turned and looked at Sara. "That was your doing?"

Sara smiled. "I'm here to help in any way I can."

"It was helpful, thank you," Alexa said, but the words came out in a begrudging tone.

Sara told Alexa that she was welcome. After taking the elevator to the basement, Sara led the way down a white-walled corridor, as her heels clacked on the polished tile floor.

"Where are we headed?" Alexa asked.

"I'm taking Tanner to see Deke Mercer," Sara said.

"That's the man who helped me clean off the paint?" Alexa asked.

"Yes."

"And he'll be working with Tanner as an armorer?"

"That's correct," Sara said.

"Good, he seemed like a nice man."

Sara laughed. "He may be nice, but I'm told he's also deadly and has forgotten more about weaponry than the three of us will ever know. It's my understanding that he's from a family of gunsmiths."

"That doesn't surprise me," Alexa said. "The man seemed… very confident."

"Um-hmm," Sara said, as she detected a note of more than admiration for Deke Mercer in Alexa's comment. Sara filed that observation away and headed toward the armory.

8
A SMILE IS WORTH A THOUSAND WORDS

When Tanner, Sara, and Alexa, entered the armory, they found Deke Mercer talking with a man named Garber.

Garber was responsible for the distribution and care of the weapons carried by the Burke Corporation's worldwide security force.

Every armed member of Burke's security team was issued a Glock 19, and it was Garber's job to keep them in good working order. Worldwide, Burke employed over four thousand security personnel, and so the task of keeping every weapon accounted for and in good working order was formidable.

Garber, who had a British accent and was a former elite soldier, had three very competent assistants who handled their jobs well. That left him with enough free time to explore his passion, which was designing and improving weapons, it was a passion that Deke Mercer shared, and he and Garber had become fast friends.

After entering the armory, Garber decided to give Tanner, Sara, and Alexa a tour of his workshop, when

Alexa noticed a weapon hung on the wall, she made an "Ooohhh," sound and headed straight for it.

The weapon looked like a dagger with a blade on each end of its handle. The blades were both double-edged and nearly a foot long, while the handle was made of the same metal as the blades but fitted for a sure grip.

"That's Deke's," Garber said, "He made it in the workshop."

Alexa looked back at Deke with a smile lighting her face. "This is a Haladie."

Deke's eyes flickered with surprise. "You know what a Haladie is?"

"Yes, they were used by the Rajput, India's ancient warriors. This looks like a real one, like the one I once saw in a museum."

"It's a copy, but real enough, would you like to hold it?"

"Of course."

Deke disengaged the straps that held the weapon to the pegboard, he then handed it to Alexa in a gentle manner.

Alexa held the weapon in her right hand as she grew accustomed to the weight of it, and its considerable heft. A few seconds later, she was making graceful thrusts at the air with it, as if she had practiced with the weapon for weeks.

Deke laughed. "You're a natural with that. Have you handled one before?"

"When I was younger I made one by welding two curved knives together. It was nothing as sleek and well-balanced as this. I found it impractical, because I could find no safe way to wear it in a sheath."

"You have a passion for edged weapons?" Deke asked.

"I do," Alexa said.

As Deke and Alexa talked, Sara was watching Tanner. The hit man showed no signs of jealousy or annoyance, but only watched the exchange with an interested gaze. Sara cleared her throat.

"Deke, I believe you had something to show Tanner, yes?"

Deke nodded at Sara and reached out to take the Haladie back from Alexa. Once the weapon was secured, Deke led them all to an indoor firing range, after Garber excused himself and returned to his desk.

On a table in the firing range was a gun carrier that was about the size of a briefcase. Deke pressed a thumb against the bio reader and the case popped open. Inside it were two guns that strongly resembled Glock 19's, but Tanner saw subtle differences that told him that they weren't. The guns had matching sound suppressors and three spare magazines each. All of it sat in fitted black foam, and the guns gleamed with their newness.

"These are for me?" Tanner asked.

"They are, but try them out. You'll find that they're different," Deke said.

"I've fired silenced guns before, Mercer."

"Not these you haven't," Deke said. "I created them myself."

Tanner removed one of the guns, checked it to see that it was unloaded, and then fed a fresh magazine into it. After threading on a sound suppressor, he took a shooting stance and aimed at the paper target that was hanging far down the range.

Tanner fired a shot that hit the target dead center, then turned and gave Deke a smile.

"The gun barely made a sound. How the hell did you do that?"

"It's a combination of the gun, the rounds, and the suppressor. They're all custom made to work together and were designed with silence in mind."

"Meaning?"

"Meaning that you'll be sacrificing distance and stopping power by using that weapon and its accompanying ammo, but anything you shoot within ten yards will die just the same."

Tanner looked down at the gun and then back at Deke. "You're an artist. I admire that."

"It's mutual, Tanner. Your killing of Alonso Alvarado was masterful. I would love to hear that whole story someday."

"Maybe Alexa will tell it to you, she killed the man alongside me. We both owed the bastard a debt of blood."

Deke stared at Alexa. "You are one interesting woman, Senorita Lucia," Deke said.

"You can call me Alexa, Mr. Mercer."

"And I'm Deke."

Sara cleared her throat once more. "Do you have anything else for Tanner, Deke?"

"No, but I would like to talk to him more; I'm sure there are items he could use. It's nice to have a real assassin to design for. It's the reason I agreed to take this position."

"I have a few ideas we could discuss," Tanner said.

Sara looked at Alexa. "Deke, why not travel to Boston with us? We'll only be there overnight, and it will give you and Tanner a chance to talk."

"Sounds good to me," Deke said.

Tanner nodded in agreement, while Alexa smiled, obviously happy to have Deke joining them on their trip.

Sara liked that smile and filed it away as another observation.

9

ASK A STUPID QUESTION...

At the start of the plane ride to Boston, Tanner and Alexa sat across from Deke and Sara.

Tanner asked Deke about his knowledge of firearms and found that it far surpassed his own, which was by no means meager. When he learned that Deke Mercer was also an explosives expert, Tanner asked him if he could put together a small charge once they were on the ground.

"I'll need to make a few purchases, but I can build you a bomb. How big a blast are we talking about?"

"Small," Tanner said. "I'll need it to blow the main circuit breaker in the underground garage."

"That's easy. I can also add a remote control so that you can detonate when you're ready."

Tanner looked over at Sara. "Recruiting Deke was your idea?"

"Yes," Sara said warily, as she wondered about Tanner's reaction.

"Excellent choice, Blake, particularly given the target I'm going after. If Adams is as hard to kill as he seems to be, I may need to use an explosives expert."

Sara smiled at him. "I'm here to help, Tanner. Remember that."

~

A SHORT TIME LATER, TANNER DECIDED TO CATCH A NAP and shut his eyes, after Deke and Sara moved off separately to take other seats on the private jet.

Sara watched with interest as Alexa left Tanner's side and settled across from Deke. From snatches of the conversation, she could hear that Alexa and Deke were discussing swords and other edged weaponry.

Sara looked for signs that Alexa was flirting but saw none. Alexa only seemed pleased to have met another enthusiast of blades.

Sara frowned. She wanted Alexa gone, as she considered her to be a distraction that Tanner didn't need.

Feeling sleepy, Sara closed her eyes for a moment. When she opened them, she found that Alexa was seated across from her. Alexa's sudden and silent appearance startled Sara, and it showed as she let out a gasp of surprise. After recovering, she asked Alexa a question.

"Can I help you?"

"Why were you staring at me?"

"You interest me."

Alexa looked Sara over as she cocked her head. "How do you mean that?"

Sara laughed. "Not sexually, although you are very attractive. My interest lies more in what Tanner sees in you. It's been my experience that the man doesn't form many close ties. Although, he has changed some in the time I've studied him."

"Studied him? You make him sound like an insect."

"When Tanner and I were enemies I studied him in

order to find a weakness in the man. Once I found that weakness, I used it against him and saved myself in the process."

"Tanner told me everything that went on between the two of you."

"Including the times we've slept together?" Sara asked.

When Alexa's mouth dropped open in shock, Sara stifled a laugh and explained.

"We shared a bed out of necessity while we were in Guambi, but of course, nothing happened."

"Why do you say, 'of course?'" Alexa asked.

Sara smiled bitterly. "It's obvious, isn't it? The man hates me."

"Tanner doesn't hate you. He wisely doesn't trust you, and for some reason he respects you, but there's no hate in his heart for you. If Tanner hated you, you'd be dead."

"Perhaps, but by becoming useful to him, I hope to end any animosity between us."

"Why does that matter to you?"

Sara shrugged. "You said that Tanner respects me; I also respect him."

Alexa stared at Sara and shook her head slightly.

"Do you want Tanner?"

Sara smiled. "Tanner said that you were psychic. If that's true, then you already know the answer to that question."

"Normally I would, but I have trouble reading you, and I don't trust you at all."

"I don't want to sleep with Tanner, Alexa."

"You want him dead."

"No, not anymore. I'm just trying to make a new life for myself inside the Burke Corporation. Working as a go-between for Tanner and the corporation is a part of my duties. Now, if you don't mind, I have work to do."

Sara opened her laptop and looked down at the screen, essentially dismissing Alexa.

Alexa stared at her a few seconds longer and then took her seat back beside Tanner, which caused him to open his eyes.

"Did you and Blake have a good talk?"

"No, and for some reason I can't read her at all."

"I haven't known Blake for very long, but I do know one thing about her."

"What's that?"

"Whenever she does anything she gives it her all."

"Even in affairs of the heart?"

"Especially in affairs of the heart. It's why her hate for me burned so bright when I killed her lover."

"And you think that the hate she felt for you just simply dissipated?"

"No, Blake killed it herself when she inadvertently caused Johnny Rossetti's death. If I had to die for killing one lover, then shouldn't she have died for causing the death of another?"

"You're talking about suicide, but she's not suicidal."

"No, but she is shut down, and she's definitely not the same woman who tried to kill me last year."

"Did you really sleep in the same bed with that bitch?"

"I see you had an interesting talk, and yes, we slept in the same bed."

"And if she had been willing, would you have had sex with her?"

"Alexa?"

"Yes?"

"I am far too skilled at survival to answer that question."

Alexa laughed and punched Tanner in the stomach

playfully. "It was a stupid question anyway. Of course, you would have slept with her."

"No comment."

"Horny bastard."

"Guilty," Tanner said.

10
DISGUSTING

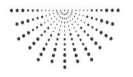

Tanner used the van to block the view of the camera in the area of the underground parking garage he was in, then left the vehicle by its sliding side door.

After picking a lock, Tanner entered the building's electrical room, where he used an adhesive to attach a small charge onto the main breaker of the electrical panel.

Deke Mercer had made the small explosive device by using parts from a garage door opener, the gunpowder from a score of bullet cartridges, and the high-voltage capacitor from a small microwave oven.

He assured Tanner that the device would destroy the circuit breaker, and thanks to the transmitter and receiver from the garage door opener, Tanner could detonate the device with a remote control.

Once the explosive was in place, Tanner locked the door on the electrical room and climbed back inside the van.

As he waited for Omar Ali Rashid and his two bodyguards to arrive, Tanner went over the plan in his head. He had been in Boston for over three hours and had spent some of that time finding a proper place to interrogate Rashid.

Sara had accompanied him as he searched, saying that she was interested in learning how he worked. Alexa didn't seem pleased that Tanner and Sara would be alone, but she wanted to stay behind and watch Deke create his bomb.

When Tanner had taken Sara to a construction site on the Charles River, she agreed that it was secluded. However, there was nothing there but muddy ground that was in the process of having a sewage system installed.

The mud was growing stiff as the temperature dropped. They were both dressed warmly, while standing on an oasis of graveled road surface.

When Sara spotted a construction trailer, she pointed at it. "Where will you torture him, in there?"

Tanner grabbed her gloved hand and moved it until she was pointing out at the expanse of muddy land.

"That's where I'll talk to him."

Sara squinted in the moonlight. "There's nothing out there but a row of portable toilets."

"Exactly," Tanner said.

Sara laughed. "Rashid is germophobic. That will be torture to him."

"Yes, and he won't dare warn Adams that I'm coming for the man, not if he ever wants to be clean again."

Sara shivered, but not from the cold. "I can just imagine what one of those toilets smell like. I'm not germophobic, but I might tell you anything you wanted to know if you stuck my head down in one of those things."

"Don't give me any ideas, Blake."

"Was that a joke?" Sara said.

"Yes."

"Good," Sara said, but she rushed back to the van.

OCCUPATION: DEATH

∽

THE LIMO ARRIVED LESS THAN AN HOUR AFTER TANNER had placed the explosive in the electrical room.

Tanner, still in the van, readied his night vision device and hit the remote control just as Rashid and his men left their limo.

The sound of the small explosion was muffled behind the closed door of the electrical room, but it had the required effect and the parking garage went dark.

The darkness wasn't complete, as the battery-powered EXIT signs cast their red glow, but the sudden loss of illumination disoriented Rashid's security guards long enough for Tanner to come up behind them unnoticed.

Tanner's sight was enhanced by the night vision monocular he wore, and he used a metal baton on the two security guards. He rendered one of the men unconscious with a blow to the side of the head, while the other man had his right kneecap broken. After disarming both men and tossing away their phones, Tanner hit a button on the van's remote and slid the side door open again.

By the time Rashid recovered from his shock and fled, it was too late. Tanner caught up to the fleeing man, grabbed him by the collar, and began dragging him toward the van. When Rashid attempted to struggle free, Tanner landed a punch into the man's gut and doubled him over.

The bodyguard with the busted knee was crawling toward Tanner and waving a short knife. The blade had been in a sheath on the guard's belt. Tanner had left it in place, thinking it to be no threat. At the time, it was a more urgent matter to nab the fleeing Rashid, rather than discard the knife.

Tanner ignored the guard long enough to blast the whimpering Rashid into silence with a stun gun. He then returned to the man with the busted knee and gave him a broken arm to go along with it. That caused the knife to fall to the ground and Tanner kicked it away.

A minute later, Rashid was bound, gagged, and being driven from the parking garage. While stopped at a traffic light, Tanner saw that the man was crying. That was good. It told Tanner that Rashid would talk.

The soft ones always did.

∼

Tanner wore tightly-laced work boots along with a pair of cheap black jeans, leather gloves, a ski mask, and a hoodie. All-together, the clothing had cost about fifty bucks.

On the other hand, Omar Ali Rashid was wearing a two-thousand-dollar suit and a pair of eight-hundred-dollar shoes. One of the shoes came off while Tanner was dragging him through the thick mud of the Boston construction site, and there wasn't enough dry cleaning in the world to save the suit from what lay in store for it.

Tanner had yet to utter a word to Rashid by the time he opened the door on the first of the green portable toilets and attempted to shove Rashid into it. The pudgy Arab resisted the attempt as if Tanner were trying to toss him into a flaming pit.

A well-placed punch to a kidney ended Rashid's struggles. Tanner dragged him inside and held his head above the reeking toilet, which contained a mixture of shit and piss from numerous donors.

There was a blue chemical in the bowl as well, but it did nothing to mask the stench. Rashid added to the vile mixture when he vomited up the remains of a lobster dinner. When he had finished retching, Tanner spoke.

"I want to know everything you know about Julien Adams, particularly his current whereabouts."

Rashid coughed, spat, and then spoke. "My brother is an important man. If you release me now and tell me who sent you, I'll tell him to let you live."

"Where is your brother?"

"He lives in New York City, but he knows people who can track you down. He is not a man you can hide from."

Tanner leaned in and whispered in Rashid's ear. "Your brother isn't here. Right now, it's just you and me."

Tanner gripped Rashid's right sleeve at the elbow and forced his bound hands down inside the toilet until they were submerged.

Rashid said, "No, no, no," in Arabic before cursing and crying. A relieved sigh followed when Tanner let him yank his arms free, but it died in his throat as Tanner gripped him by the hair and began pushing his face toward the toilet bowl.

After a yelp of terror, Rashid shouted Adams location. His voice echoed with a hollow tone from the confines of the toilet.

"Greece! Julien Adams is on a private island off the coast of Greece."

Tanner interrogated Rashid for another ten minutes and became certain that the man had told him everything he knew about Julien Adams.

Tanner gave Rashid another blast of the stun gun before walking a short distance away to call Sara and give her the information.

She informed him that Burke personnel in Greece would be able to keep the island under surveillance and would begin issuing regular reports by morning. She would also coordinate with them for a place to work out of, and it would all be ready by the time they landed in the country.

"How soon can we get a flight to Greece?" Tanner asked Sara.

"I'll have a jet ready to leave by eight a.m., and Tanner?"

"Yes?"

"Is Rashid still alive?"

"Yes, Blake. I don't kill when I don't have to."

"And was it really necessary to kill that guard earlier at the Burke Corporate Campus?"

"Yes."

"Why?"

"It set a tone. Sloane Lennox was attempting to set the tone with his stupid test, and I reset it by killing that guard. I'm not one of Burke's employees. I want that understood from day one."

"You're the best killer on the planet and they're lucky to have your services."

There was a pause, and then Tanner spoke.

"Are you mocking me, Blake?"

"No Tanner, I was simply stating a fact. Even when I wanted to kill you I never doubted your abilities; it's why I lobbied so hard to have you work with us."

"Lennox had someone else in mind, didn't he?"

"Yes."

"Who?"

"That Sicilian, Scallato."

"Maurice Scallato, yes, Julien Adams wouldn't survive him either."

"You know Scallato?"

"By reputation only," Tanner said, as he caught movement from the corner of his eye and saw that Rashid had recovered from the blast and was crying again. "I have to go, Blake, but I'll be back soon."

"Goodbye, Tanner. I'll meet you in the hotel lobby after seven a.m."

"Fine."

Before leaving the construction site, Tanner promised Rashid that he would kill him painfully if he were to warn Adams. Rashid said that he owed Adams nothing and cursed the day he'd met him.

Tanner stunned Rashid with an elbow to the side of his head, gripped him with both hands, and dunked him headfirst into the muck of the toilet, but just deep enough to immerse the man's hair.

"Warn Adams or attempt to seek revenge and I'll drown you in something that will make this smell sweet."

Tanner left Rashid sobbing inside the toilet, trod through the mud, and drove off into the night.

Tanner knew where to find Adams. Now came the hard part, killing the man.

11

FOOD FOR THOUGHT

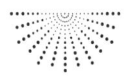

One of the Burke Corporation's Gulfstream jets flew at over five-hundred miles an hour, as it winged its way to Rhodes, Greece.

Aboard the luxury jet were Tanner, Alexa, Sara, Deke Mercer, and Garber. Garber was the head of the armory and a man who had once been a member of the British Special Forces, the SAS.

Garber spent the flight either asleep or on the phone with his wife, who was six months pregnant. Garber was unaware of the true purpose of the trip, although he could certainly guess. Deke assured Tanner and Sara that Garber was trustworthy, and also needed, as he possessed an expertise that Deke didn't.

"What would that be?" Tanner asked.

"Sea craft, personal sea craft to be more accurate. You'll need a way to get on and off the island. With the security that Adams has in place, you'll have to be stealthy about it."

"I've done some scuba diving; I thought that I would just swim in underwater," Tanner said.

Deke shook his head. "We'll hook you up with something better. If the shit hits the fan, you'll need to move fast."

"I don't plan to fail, Deke," Tanner said.

"I get that. But it's my job to help you, and part of helping you will be to plan for a retreat."

Alexa smiled at Deke. "You have something in mind?"

"Yes, a Seabob water sled. Have you ever used one, Tanner?"

"No, but they're like an underwater jet ski, correct?"

"Yes, and once we get to Greece, Garber there will train you in the use of one. The Seabob will help you get on and off the island much faster than swimming, and because it works underwater you'll have less chance of being spotted."

Sara let out a sigh and showed Tanner her phone. "That's the preliminary report from our surveillance. Adams hasn't been spotted, but there are at least sixteen armed guards and several servants. There are also three guard towers. The towers are all temporary structures, but they offer the guards a good view."

"How big is this island?" Tanner asked.

Sara fiddled with her phone and brought up an aerial view. "As you can see it's very small. The house and the surrounding servant quarters take up nearly half of the useable land. Adams has three fast boats standing by. My guess is that once he knows he's in danger he'll take off in one of them, which one he'll use would be anyone's guess."

Tanner studied the aerial view and made a comment. "I'm surprised the government doesn't send in a commando team."

"That's a private island on Greek soil," Sara said. "As much as our government wants Adams dead, they don't want to advertise to the world that a prominent American is engaged in terrorist activities."

"Once I get on that island he'll no longer be involved in anything, including breathing," Tanner said.

∿

After landing at Rhodes International Airport, Tanner and the others were taken to an estate in Paradisi, Greece. The estate was on the water and had its own private white sand beach, along with a dock and a sailboat.

Tanner and Alexi's accommodations were large and well-appointed, as was Sara's room, which was across the hall. After unpacking, showering, and changing, Tanner went in search of Garber.

There were still a few hours of daylight left when they arrived in Greece. On the limo ride to the house from the airport, Tanner asked Garber if he could give him his first lesson on the underwater craft.

"I'll do better than that, sir. If you're willing we can continue your training all evening, after all, you'll be using the Seabob at night."

"Good point, Garber, and just call me Tanner, I'm nobody's sir."

Garber looked over at Deke. "You're right, he's a regular bloke."

"Do you have to deal with a lot of assholes, Garber?" Tanner asked.

Garber shrugged. "The corporate types all like to be called sir or ma'am."

"That doesn't apply to me," Sara said.

Garber grinned at her. "Not yet, but if you stay at Burke long enough, you'll become infected."

Tanner found Deke and Garber in the four-car garage that had been converted into a staging area for the assault on Adams' island.

There were two Seabobs, and Garber and Deke were already busy modifying them to be as silent as possible. Both men were dressed in swim trunks, as was Tanner, who was eager to get his first lesson on the Seabob.

Sara walked through the doorway that connected the house to the garage. She was dressed in a white bikini, but also wore a translucent red beach robe, which was unfastened. Alexa followed behind her, wearing a very flattering, and revealing, one-piece bathing suit.

Both Deke and Garber stared openly at the women with admiring stares.

"You ladies look lovely," Deke said. "I take it you'll be joining us on the beach?"

Alexa nodded as she stared back at Deke. A look of concern flashed across her face as she took in the scar from a healed wound on Deke's left side, beneath the ribs.

"That's a nasty knife wound."

Deke raised his arm and looked at it.

"I was careless once."

"In combat?" Alexa asked.

"Yes," Deke said, but didn't elaborate. He then pointed over at Tanner and referred to the old scar on Tanner's chest. "I've never seen anyone who was hit there get back up. You must have been very lucky."

"I was," Tanner said, as Sara moved closer and studied the healed wound.

"I've wondered about this old scar," she said, and then touched it lightly, almost as a caress, while looking up into Tanner's eyes. "Who did this to you?"

"Alonso Alvarado."

"Alvarado? I guess you two had some history?"

"We did."

"He failed to kill you and you eventually killed him."

"Something to keep in mind," Alexa said, as Sara took her hand from Tanner's chest.

"Are we ready to begin, Garber?" Tanner asked.

"We are."

"Then let's get to it. I plan to make my move tomorrow night."

∽

TANNER, WHILE NATURALLY ATHLETIC, TURNED OUT NOT TO be a natural when it came to being adept at using the Seabob. He was fine while the craft moved straight, but had trouble handling quick course changes.

It frustrated him, as he had always been swift at mastering new skills. It wasn't enough that he be good with the machine, he needed to be expert with it, as he would be using it at night, in almost total darkness.

Deke and Garber had equipped the Seabobs with subdued headlights, but they only gave illumination out to a dozen yards or so.

They had no way of knowing what might be in the water surrounding Adams' island, such as old shipwrecks, garbage, or unusual coral formations. If Tanner came upon an obstacle and couldn't avoid a collision with it, his attack on the island could end before he ever stepped on shore.

Garber proved to be a patient instructor, and he and Tanner continued training well after everyone else had gone to bed. There was a nearly full moon and the Seabobs had lights, but Garber set up several ultra-bright work lights and aimed them at the water. They provided just enough visibility underwater for Tanner to keep training.

He and Garber were still going at it at dawn, but by then, Tanner was highly proficient at handling the underwater sea craft.

"Oh my God, have you two been out here all night?" Sara asked, as she walked over to them. She was barefoot and wearing denim shorts with a red, sleeveless top.

"It took all night for me to get the hang of it," Tanner said. "But thanks to Garber, I'll be ready to hit the island tonight."

"Excellent," Sara said, and then she followed Tanner and Garber back to the garage, where they sat the Seabobs on top of a bench, then stowed away the lights.

Deke was already up and at work. He told Tanner he would have both machines refueled and ready to go by nightfall. When Alexa came downstairs a few minutes later, everyone went into the kitchen for breakfast.

There were no servants at the estate so that they could have their privacy, however, the refrigerator and pantry were fully stocked. To the surprise of everyone, Sara volunteered to cook.

"I thought you grew up in a house full of servants, Blake?" Tanner said.

"I did, and one of them taught me to cook. I'm no chef, but I do know how to prepare breakfast."

"Would you like some help?" Alexa asked.

Sara stared at her for a moment, but then nodded her head. "Sure, help would be nice."

To Tanner's surprise, Sara and Alexa seemed to get along better as they prepared breakfast. He had gone up to his room for a quick shower and when he returned, he found the women laughing together over something as they made breakfast burritos. It pleased Tanner to see them getting along and he hoped it would continue. As long as they all had to be together, they might as well make the best of it.

As Alexa placed the food on the table and poured coffee, Sara made short work of the pots and pans used to prepare the meal, then everyone settled at the table to eat.

Tanner and Garber were ravenous from the hours they'd spent in the water overnight, and the two of them ate most of the food that the women had prepared. Alexa had worried that they had made too much, but the food disappeared quickly.

"This food is excellent," Tanner said between bites.

"You can thank Alexa," Sara said. "She taught me a thing or two about using spices and my eggs have never tasted better."

"It was a team effort," Alexa said.

"I'll take care of dinner, ladies," Deke said.

Alexa smiled at Deke. "You can cook?"

"Oh, hell no, I can barely heat up an army MRE, but I'll buy dinner for everyone while I'm out seeing the sights later."

Garber let out a yawn as he stood. "I'll be catching up on my sleep today, but I could go for some really good moussaka for dinner."

"You got it," Deke said, "Any other requests?"

Everyone else agreed that moussaka sounded good along with gyros and other native Greek dishes.

After Garber went upstairs, Tanner kissed Alexa and told her he was going to get some sleep as well.

"While I'm resting, why don't you go out and see the sights."

"You're welcome to tag along with me, Alexa," Deke said.

Alexa considered it for a moment and then agreed to join Deke. Afterwards, she looked over at Sara. "Will you be coming along?"

"I'd love to, but I have to stay here and make a few calls. I want to be certain that Tanner has the latest intel when he makes his move on the island tonight."

Alexa looked at Tanner. "I wish you could come with us, but I know that you need your rest."

"Don't worry about me, just have a good time," Tanner said.

Alexa gave him a kiss and then she and Deke headed out to see the sights, but before leaving the home, they both went up to their rooms. Alexa needed her purse, while Deke wanted to grab his camera.

Sara smiled at Tanner as he rose from the table to head off to sleep. "Get plenty of rest, Tanner. You'll be having a busy night."

"If all goes well, Julien Adams will be dead this time tomorrow."

"And will you accept another assignment with Burke if one comes up?"

"Let's wait and see how this one turns out."

"Fair enough," Sara said, and then she walked out to sit on the home's rear deck while Tanner climbed the stairs to go to his room.

The sound of laughter reached Sara's ears and she walked to the edge of the deck and saw Alexa and Deke climbing into a Jeep with an open top. The vehicle came with the house, along with an old Volvo. Alexa and Deke were laughing about something and seemed to be getting along very well.

Sara went back to her seat and stared out at the ceaseless waves crashing upon the shore. On her face was a wide smile.

12

SUICIDE TRUMPS MURDER

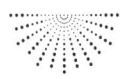

Sara finished with work earlier than she thought she would and decided to travel toward the docks to explore Mandraki Harbor. While walking about the shops there, she hoped to get a glimpse of Alexa and Deke together.

Alexa liked Deke, and anyone could see that it was mutual. Sara hoped that the friendship would grow into something more and cause Tanner to cut Alexa out of his life. Tanner didn't need to be distracted by a girlfriend. He needed to keep his mind on his mission and Sara saw Alexa as a threat to that.

Sara frowned as she thought about Tanner and Alexa's relationship. They seemed close, very close. That surprised Sara, who at one time had thought that Tanner was a sociopath incapable of having feelings.

Tanner had been in love with Laurel Ivy. Would he now fall in love with Alexa? Sara didn't think so, but the last thing Tanner needed was a wife to worry about. That sort of emotional involvement would change the man, make him lose his edge, and possibly get him killed.

Sara needed Tanner alive and killing. She had brought him into Burke's government-sanctioned wet works program, and he was her responsibility. If Tanner did well, Sara would do well too.

Sara failed to come across Alexa and Deke but did spy another familiar face. It was a man who had been her lover years ago, when she first joined the Bureau. She wondered what he was doing in Greece.

The man's name was Cole McManus and he was a CIA agent, or at least he had been years earlier. At the moment, he appeared to be a deck hand on a huge yacht named the Sea Beast and was polishing a brass railing.

Sara was about to walk over and talk to him when she saw another man on the boat call to Cole. However, the man didn't call Cole by his real name.

"Shamus, when you get done with that, head on over to the fish shop and pick up our order."

Sara saw Cole wave in acknowledgment to the man before getting back to work. The fact that Cole was using an alias told her that he was likely working undercover. She moved back into the crowd of shoppers before Cole could spot her.

The near encounter had her thinking of the past and her years as a federal agent. That life was behind her now. She needed to look forward and concentrate on building a future at Burke.

She silently wished Cole McManus luck and headed back toward the house, back to Tanner.

∽

Tanner awoke in time for dinner and then Garber gave him one more training session with the Seabob. Tanner handled the machine with confidence. When midnight came, everyone climbed aboard the sailboat and headed for the island where Adams was hiding out.

Garber killed the engine on the boat when they were nearing the island, as Alexa and Deke helped Tanner with his gear. Garber had dropped anchor behind a nearby atoll that was just big enough to shield the boat from the view of anyone on Adams' island.

He would be running the boat with lights off when it was time to take Tanner closer, and wore a night vision monocular that was a twin of the one Tanner was equipped with.

Tanner would don a small tank of air that he would leave beside the Seabob once he reached the island. There was also a set of specialized goggles, and one of Deke's silenced guns dangled from Tanner's waist in a water-proof pouch.

When Deke secured a second smaller pouch onto Tanner, he asked the armorer what it was.

"It's insurance," Deke said, and then went on to explain its purpose to Tanner.

After lowering himself over the side with the Seabob, Tanner sent Alexa a wink and headed toward the island. He would be traveling most of the way there while fifty feet below the surface and traveling at a speed of five miles an hour.

As Garber moved the boat around to the pick-up location, Alexa turned from looking down into the dark water and stared at Sara.

"What happens if he's captured?"

"He won't be," Sara said.

Alexa smiled and nodded to herself. "Of course, he's a Tanner. He'll survive no matter what."

"A *Tanner*, as in there are more than one?"

"He's the seventh Tanner; I thought that you knew that?"

"I was aware that there had been others who took the name; I wasn't certain that it was a legacy type of thing."

"Tanner is the best killer in the world because he was trained by the best killer in the world and has the accumulated knowledge of all the Tanners who came before him."

Sara settled into a deck chair and gestured for Alexa to take the one beside her.

"Tell me about the Tanners. It will help to keep you from worrying about him."

Alexa was staring at the lights of the island, but then settled beside Sara.

"From what I understand, the first Tanner took the name almost a hundred years ago. It seems he had been a soldier in World War I and…"

As Alexa told Sara about the legend of the Tanners, Sara listened with rapt attention.

~

MEANWHILE, TANNER REALIZED HE WAS GROWING CLOSER to the island's shoreline and cut the power on the Seabob.

When he was close enough to stand neck deep in the waves, he saw that he had hit the position he was going for, thanks to the illuminated compass that Deke had secured to the Seabob. Tanner was a hundred feet away from the guard tower on the far left, while the house loomed up beyond the tower. Tanner would head for the house once he took out the tower guard.

The guard was either an amateur or a fool because the man was smoking. After moving closer, Tanner aimed his silenced gun to a spot three inches above the glow of the man's cigarette. The gun's near silence impressed Tanner once more as he fired two rounds into the guard's skull. The man's head jerked backwards before he crumpled and fell onto the floor of the guard tower.

The word, tower, was an overstatement as the stand was more the height of a lifeguard station than a traditional guard tower. Still, the structure contained a searchlight and a siren. Tanner disabled both pieces of equipment after making certain the guard was dead.

He also removed the man's radio and cell phone, which he tossed back into the waves, not far from the spot on the shore where he'd left the Seabob.

With the first guard handled, Tanner headed toward the house and approached it from the side. His plan was to stay undetected for as long as possible. Thanks to the mole in Adams' organization, Tanner knew that Adams was a night owl and would stay up until early in the morning, while sleeping away the day. That meant that the man would be awake and moving about, so catching him asleep was unlikely.

Tanner took a position among the foliage near the edge of the patio and stared in at a sun room. The room was empty, but Tanner observed a servant walking by in the adjacent hallway. The man was carrying a tray with a bottle and a glass on it.

The servant was young and looked Indian. Tanner wouldn't kill the servants unless he had to. In his experience, anyone not in the line of fire would run at the first sight of a gun anyway.

The guards wouldn't run though, and Tanner would kill them. A dead guard was one less threat to face on the way back to the shore after the hit was completed.

The lock on the patio door offered little resistance and had no alarm to disable. Tanner was soon inside the home.

He left the sun room and walked along the route that the servant had taken, hoping that it would lead him to Adams.

There was no sign of the servant or of anyone else on the ground floor, while the door leading to a small rear section of the house was locked. Tanner suspected that it was a room used by the guards. It was in a corner of the home and had a slot for a key card.

Tanner had already passed Adams' empty office while exploring the home and assumed that the man was on an upper floor. The home had an elevator, but it also required a key card.

When Tanner came to a staircase, he saw that there was a camera pointed at it. He knew that if he attempted to disable it he would alert the guards anyway, and so he ignored it and boldly rushed up the stairs.

He reached the second floor just as the servant he had spotted earlier came out of a room with an empty serving tray. Tanner came up on the man in a rush just as an alarm sounded.

An elbow to the throat dropped the servant to the carpeted floor of the hallway, then Tanner shot the lock on the door the servant had just passed through. He entered the room just in time to see Adams climb out of a bed that contained a blonde woman who was half his age. The woman was naked, while Adams was wearing a pair of boxers.

Adams turned and sprinted toward a door at the rear of the room. Tanner had the man in his sights and was about to kill him when the blonde screamed out a cry of fury and rushed toward Tanner. The naked young woman was beautiful, but she had a look of desperation in her eyes and was blocking Tanner's view of Adams.

Tanner pointed the gun at the woman's face, expecting

her to turn or cower in fear, but instead she kept coming and collided into him and nearly knocked him over. When Tanner went to push her away with his gun arm, the woman gripped the silencer and pressed it against her head.

The act shocked Tanner, but he was even more surprised when the girl tried to wedge a finger against the trigger. She was trying to kill herself while also protecting Adams. Meanwhile, Adams had made it through the door and bolted it shut from the other side. Tanner had only caught a brief glimpse of the interior but thought that the room was a vault or a safe room.

Tanner overcame his shock and broke free of the woman, as the sound of heavy feet pounding on the stairs could be heard.

Tanner let out a loud curse as he decided to abort this attempt at killing Adams and placed his attention on escaping. He slapped the blonde senseless, lowered her onto the floor a few feet in front of the door, then spread her legs wide.

With its broken lock, the door offered the guards no resistance and four of them flooded into the room.

As they caught sight of the naked blonde with her thighs spread, all four men froze and stared at the area between her legs.

They stared for only an instant, but that instant was enough. Tanner emptied a magazine into the men's backs and sides from where he was concealed at the side of a dresser.

Although fatally wounded, two of the guards returned fire before falling to the floor. Their shots passed through the oak wood of the dresser as if it weren't there. One of their shots hit home and caught Tanner on the side of his left forearm as he was reloading.

Tanner was bringing up the gun to fire again when the blonde regained her senses and reached for one of the guards fallen weapons. He thought he would have to kill her as well, but the woman placed the gun against her chest and pulled the trigger.

Despite hearing voices coming from the foot of the steps, Tanner took the time to talk to the girl as she lay dying. He saw that she was in her mid-teens, but that her make-up made her look older.

"Why did you kill yourself?"

The wounded girl answered him in English that had a strong Slavic accent.

"My family will be taken care of now, and I'll be free… free…"

Tanner laid her flat on the carpet as her eyes closed. He then sent several shots out into the hallway as he hoped to buy time for his escape.

The bedroom contained a balcony. Tanner, in a burst of adrenaline and urgent desire, dragged the mattress off the bed, onto the balcony, and flipped it over the waist high marble railing.

He was standing on that railing preparing to jump when a guard fired from the doorway and shot him in the back, striking him just beneath his right shoulder.

Tanner was clad in a wet suit that had lightweight body armor incorporated into it. The armor did its job and kept the slug from entering Tanner's back. However, he still felt as if he'd been hit with a sledgehammer. The impact of the shot had knocked him off balance, and he found himself falling headfirst toward the mattress sixteen feet below.

Tanner managed to turn in midair but not quickly enough to land on his feet. After hitting the mattress while falling on his butt, he stood, stumbled, rolled, and slammed into the side of the home while hitting his head.

A sudden darkness swam behind his eyes and threatened to swallow him. Tanner fought it, knowing that if he gave in to the blackness, he might never see light again. And as he fought to remain conscious, Adams' remaining guards were closing in on his position.

The hit had gone wrong, Adams was alive, and now it was just a struggle to stay alive. Tanner fought off the darkness, pulled himself upright, and looked about for a way to survive.

13
ROUND ONE

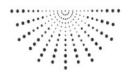

Alexa had been telling Sara about the legend of the Tanners when the faint sound of gunfire carried to their ears.

"That sounds like trouble," Sara said.

They were at the rendezvous position, which was a thousand yards to the west of where Tanner went into the water. The change had also brought them closer to the island and Tanner was to swim back out to them.

Sara rose, then lowered a waterproof lantern over the side of the boat and beneath the water, so that its glow would guide Tanner to their position. The Seabob had an oversized illuminated compass that would also guide him to the boat.

Alexa borrowed Garber's night vision monocular and searched the shore for Tanner. She could only make out green shadowy figures moving about. And because of the swell of the waves, they were only viewed from the waist up.

Alexa spoke to Sara as Deke joined them. "We should move closer."

"No," Sara said. "Tanner has these coordinates; if we move, we could pass him without knowing it."

Alexa wanted to argue but knew that Sara was right. She searched the shoreline again and saw that one of the guards was scanning the sea, as he tried to locate their vessel. The guard likely had his own night vision in the rifle scope he was using. And judging by the size of his rifle, their boat might be in range.

"One of the guards is searching for us with a rifle scope," Alexa said. "He must realize that Tanner had to have arrived by boat."

Deke moved up beside her and held up something that looked like a TV remote.

"What's that?" Alexa asked.

Deke smiled at her as he pressed a button. "This is a diversion."

A bright light flared from the area where they had been when Tanner went into the water. The guard with the rifle looked startled and then fired several rounds at the light, which was blinding.

Sara smiled. "That will not only make them believe that we're over there, but they'll also assume that Tanner will be leaving from the shoreline that's aligned with that position. Good work, Deke."

"Thanks boss. But what about Tanner, do you think he's okay?"

"Absolutely," Sara said. "The man is indestructible. Tell Garber to hold this position even if we take fire."

"All right, but you ladies might want to go below into the cabin."

"No," Alexa said. "Tanner may need help climbing back in."

"Do we have any way to defend ourselves if we're fired upon?" Sara asked Deke.

Deke grinned at her. "I'm a Marine, remember? I've got a rifle ready to go."

Alexa dropped to her knees and peered down into the dark water, looking for any sign of Tanner. What she didn't realize, was that Tanner had yet to leave the island.

∼

After staving off unconsciousness and regaining his balance, Tanner saw the silhouettes of three guards drawing closer. The men were approaching his position while walking several feet apart and with their rifles raised and ready to fire.

Thanks to his black wet suit, they had yet to spot him where he crouched at the base of a wall amid the plants. Tanner decided that it was time to use one of the items Deke had placed in the extra pouch.

It was a homemade grenade that was basically a short pipe bomb. The thing was rigged with a push button fuse that Deke told Tanner was set to blow after five seconds passed. Tanner was closer to the men than he'd like to be when the blast went off but was willing to risk it. He pressed down on the button, waited two seconds, and lobbed the grenade toward the guard in the middle.

The contraption landed at the man's feet and exploded an instant later. The guard in the middle was killed, as several nails tore into his flesh, while the men walking beside him suffered injuries to their legs and abdomens.

After tossing the grenade, Tanner had dropped to the ground. As he rose back up, he saw that the wall behind him had received two nails at about waist level. Tanner sprinted away from the men, who were screaming in pain, and headed back toward the shoreline, where he had killed the tower guard.

The Seabob was where he had stowed it, at the base of the tower, along with the air tank. To his left, a tower guard was firing out at sea toward a light he took to be coming from a boat. It was another of Deke's tricks. Once again, Tanner was glad to have the man on his side.

Tanner ignored the air tank and stepped into the water with the Seabob. There was no time to strap the tank on, as he could make out several shapes running toward him. As the first shots came his way, he fired back and was rewarded with the sound of one of the men grunting in pain and falling to the sand.

"Kill that bastard!" the man told the guards with him, as Tanner waded into the surf with the Seabob.

It was time to use the second item Deke had placed in the pouch. It was a balloon sheathed inside several other balloons and filled with concentrated red food dye. Once he was in the water, Tanner squeezed the balloon until it burst open and was surprised by how much it resembled blood, as it mixed with the seawater in the near darkness.

As Tanner dived beneath the waves with the Seabob, a bullet struck its covering, just above one of the handles, and damaged the compass. That wasn't good, but at least the slug didn't cause any damage to the Seabob's engine.

Once he was well beneath the surface of the water, Tanner saw two more bullets pass by on the left, amid the glow of the Seabob's headlight. The rounds moved in a strange slow motion, and Tanner wondered if they would even pierce his skin had they struck him.

If Deke's blood balloon worked the way they hoped it would, the guards at the shoreline would think that Tanner had received a serious wound and was bleeding heavily. That would give them less incentive to keep firing while making them believe he might be dead.

Tanner was bleeding, as the shot that struck his

forearm had ripped his flesh open, but Tanner felt fortunate that the bullet had done so little damage. An inch to the right and he would have a broken arm at the very least.

Tanner stayed under for as long as he could and then surfaced for air. No one fired at him, and it looked as if the guard shooting at the light had ceased doing so. After regaining his breath, Tanner dived with the Seabob once again. Before coming up for air the second time, he had spotted the glow of the lantern far to his left.

Without the compass to guide him, he had been drifting off course. Tanner dived once again and headed for the glow of the underwater lantern. He nearly made it all the way to the boat but had to surface for air a dozen feet away.

He saw Sara staring at him and noticed that she looked relieved to see him. That relief morphed into a look of concern when she saw the wound on his forearm.

"Were you shot?"

"Yes, but not seriously," Tanner answered as he moved to the side of the boat.

As Sara took the Seabob from him, Alexa and Deke helped him aboard.

Tanner sat in the boat and looked up at them.

"Adams is still alive. I'll have to try again."

Sara leaned over and stared into his eyes. "You'll kill him."

"Yes."

Sara straightened and called over to Garber, who was at the wheel. "Take us back. It's time to regroup."

Garber nodded, started the engines, and pointed the boat back toward their private beach.

Round one had ended.

14

ROUND TWO

Tanner saw the looks of bewilderment on the faces of Alexa, Sara, and Deke as he told them about the girl who attacked him and killed herself.

They were in the room Tanner shared with Alexa, and Alexa was bandaging Tanner's wounded forearm. He also had an ugly bruise on his back where the slug had hit the body armor.

When Sara looked as if a light had suddenly gone off in her head, Tanner asked her what she was thinking.

"What you said about the girl attacking you, something similar occurred while I was still with the Bureau. I was part of a joint taskforce sent to arrest a man suspected of running a gang of white slavers. After entering the house, we found three naked women chained up in the basement. The women attacked us as we tried to free them, and one even grabbed an agent's gun and attempted to shoot herself."

"Why?" Alexa asked.

"The girls were told that if they ever escaped and went to the police that their families would be killed. On the other hand, if they died defending their owners or killed themselves instead of being apprehended or questioned by the authorities, then their families would receive a large sum of money. It was all a lie of course, but their fear for their families kept them in line, while their love for them made suicide seem attractive."

"Why would anyone believe that?" Deke asked.

Sara made a face of disgust. "All three of the girls were no more than sixteen and they had been taken from their families when they were just children. The slavers brainwashed them into believing their lies and converted them into being another line of defense."

"It worked for Adams," Tanner said. "If not for the girl, he'd be dead right now. She delayed me long enough for him to reach his safe room."

"I have to report in to Mr. Burke, Tanner. How long will it be until you make a second attempt?"

"I'll be hitting them again... tonight."

"What?" Alexa and Sara asked at the same time.

"You heard me right. I need to hit them right away; they won't be expecting it and won't have time to recruit new guards."

Sara shook her head. "No. We'll wait and plan out another attack. Everyone on that island is on edge right now and they'll likely shoot you the second you step foot on it."

"I wasn't asking for permission, Blake; I was just telling you what I'm going to do."

"It sounds foolish," Sara said.

Alexa appeared to be as upset as Sara was, but she calmly took Tanner's hand in her own.

"Why do you want to attack again so soon?"

"I'll go in just before dawn, just as the first faint glow is seen in the east. Their guard will be down then, and they'll have been awake all night."

"You'll have to go in harder," Deke said, and Tanner agreed.

"You're right, the time for stealth is done. I have to blitz them. You wouldn't happen to have a rocket launcher lying around, would you?"

"I have something even better, an M32. I had it shipped ahead in pieces, but I can reassemble it in no time."

Tanner assumed that Deke was joking, but then realized he was serious.

"An M32 will make a second assault easy," Tanner said.

"What's an M32?" Alexa said, and to the surprise of Tanner and Deke, Sara answered her.

"It's basically a rifle that fires grenades like a six-shooter. It's also something I never requisitioned."

"It's my own property, boss. It's disassembled and lying inside a crate in the garage, but I can have it back together in minutes."

Tanner stood up from the bed and looked at his freshly bandaged arm before speaking to Deke.

"You realize that I may have to abandon the M32 after it's empty?"

"I do," Deke said, "That's why the boss lady here will promise me a new one in any event."

Sara nodded. "I'll talk to Mr. Burke, and don't call me boss lady, my name is Sara."

"Whatever you say, Sara," Deke said.

Garber appeared in the doorway. "The Seabob has a cracked casing, but we still have the other one."

"That's good," Tanner said. "Now let's get ready for round two."

A FEW SHORT HOURS LATER, SARA STOOD BESIDE DEKE AT the wheel of the boat and watched Tanner and Alexa as they said goodbye again.

Sara marveled at Tanner's calmness. The man had even caught a short nap before they left the house and now he was headed back to an island where he had been lucky to escape the first time.

A Tanner, Sara thought, and reasoned that the main trait each Tanner must look for in a protégée was fearlessness. That was something that couldn't be taught, was beyond rare, and an attribute that Tanner possessed in spades.

Nothing ever seemed to bother the man, although he had to have witnessed more violence in his life than most combat veterans. His psyche must be such that he could simply push aside those things that others would dwell on, and in most men would spawn nightmares, or shackle them with a post-traumatic stress disorder.

While seeking revenge against him, Sara had found it necessary to ignore Tanner's positive attributes and to dehumanize him by thinking of him as a monster, a mere killing machine, or a heartless psychopath.

With her mind cleared of vengeance, and her association with Tanner more personal, Sara had come to see him for what he was. Tanner was an exceptional man, and one whose chosen occupation was death, and the delivering of it to others.

It also had not escaped her notice that she found him to be attractive, even sexy, although she'd never admit it to anyone but herself. His confidence bordered on egotism at times, but it was based in reality. Tanner was every bit as good as he thought he was, Sara knew, and damn if that didn't just make the man seem hotter.

∼

Tanner gave Alexa a parting kiss, then stared over at Sara. She walked up to him and offered her hand.

"Good luck, Tanner, and come back in one piece."

"That's the plan," Tanner said.

After Tanner lowered himself into the water, Deke handed down the Seabob, as well as the watertight bag containing the M32. With that done, Deke pointed toward his newest creation. It was a mannequin he had come across while exploring the house. Deke had put a wet suit on it and dropped it in the water earlier. After checking with a pair of binoculars, it appeared to be headed to shore.

"Our friend is moving in with the tide, Tanner."

"Good, that should buy me a few seconds of distraction and allow me to get close to the house. I have to keep Adams from running into his safe room again."

Alexa sent Tanner a little wave. "I'll be waiting for you."

"I'll be right back," Tanner said, as he turned on the Seabob. Seconds later, he was under the water and headed back into danger.

It was where he had lived most of his life.

15

HE AIN'T NO HO

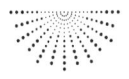

Darren Grimes was tired.

As a part of Adams security team, the young mercenary had been up all night to guard against another attack and was given the duty of patrolling the shoreline near the house.

The bastard who had tried to kill Adams earlier had wiped out half of them. Now they had to keep Adams alive long enough to get him off the island in one piece.

At least the guy that tried to hit Adams was thought to be dead. Anyway, that was the story going around, since one of the other guards said that there was a lot of blood in the water where the guy went in.

Darren sighed. The girl Adams had been banging had died in the attack. Darren had liked the girl, who had been named Karla. Karla had been bought and paid for by Adams. She had been a whore most of her short life and Darren thought that sucked, but the world was what it was and hot little things like Karla became property of men all the time, one way or another.

Darren chuckled to himself. Wasn't he a whore too?

He sold his ass to Adams for two grand a week and nearly got killed doing so on more than one occasion.

It was like that old saying—In this world, you're either a pimp or a ho.

Darren was halfway through a yawn when he spotted something bobbing in the surf. He couldn't be certain, but from the shape of the object he thought it might be a man. He unslung the AR-15 he had hanging across his back and looked through his scope.

The optics on the gun weren't great, seeing as they lacked night vision, but the sun was lending a glow as it peeked above the horizon. Darren saw what looked like a man floating face down in the surf.

He opened his mouth to raise the alarm but then shut it. What he was seeing wasn't moving. It was likely the body of the dude that had attacked them earlier. They had thought that the body must have been washed out to sea, but the waves in their fickleness must have brought the corpse back.

Darren waded into the water until he was standing knee deep and then waited for the body to come to him. He realized what it was before it even reached him and wondered where it had come from.

It was a mannequin in a wet suit and goggles. Darren dragged it out of the water and was looking into the lens of the goggles when he saw movement reflected in them. Before he could react, he felt the knife slide between his ribs and he experienced a moment of intense agony that made his eyes water.

Darren fell to his knees, then onto his back in the wet sand, where he stared up at his attacker.

The man had the eyes of a predator. Besides the bloody knife he held, he was also holding one of the biggest goddamn guns that Darren had ever seen.

"You are definitely a pimp," Darren mumbled, and then he died, as his punctured heart ceased sending blood to his brain.

∽

Tanner stepped over Darren's corpse and ran toward the guard tower that was nearest to Adams' house. When he was a hundred yards away, Tanner stopped running and fired off a grenade. The guard had spotted his approach and was already firing at him, but the two shots he was able to squeeze off went wide of Tanner.

The 40-mm grenade also went wide of its target and landed in the sand several feet away from the guard tower. Tanner hadn't fired an M32 in over a decade and his skill with the weapon was rusty, but he remembered that at close range you had to aim the sights low, as the gun was designed to hit targets that were hundreds of meters away. Still, the blast went off close enough to topple the guard tower and kill the guard.

With that accomplished, Tanner launched two grenades toward the house. Both grenades were fired at the balcony he had leapt from earlier, beyond which laid not only Adams' bedroom, but also the safe room that the man had fled into, to avoid Tanner. Once again, Tanner had to aim low or he risked having the grenades sailing over the house.

The mattress he had landed on earlier was gone from the lawn, but Tanner took aim at the room it had come from, and the grenade sailed through the balcony doors and lit up Adams' bedroom.

If anyone were inside that room they would be dead, but Tanner fired a second grenade to cause structural damage to the room.

Tanner hoped that the twin blasts would kill Adams, but if they failed to accomplish that, then they should keep him from reaching his safe room. When fire and smoke erupted from the room beyond the balcony, Tanner felt that he had effectively stopped Adams from sheltering himself behind a steel reinforced door.

If the man had never left the safe room after the earlier attack, then the fresh debris would keep him trapped inside until Tanner could breach the door and kill him. Tanner's wish was that the man had died in the blasts, and it was time to verify the kill.

Sirens blared, and men were running in Tanner's direction. He sent his fourth grenade at the herd running toward him, even as one of their shots struck him in the chest. The shot was stopped by the body armor Tanner wore, but its impact was brutal and caused him to not only drop to his knees in agony, but it also affected his aim and made it falter.

The grenade struck the ground too far in front of the guards to kill any of them but did send a blast of sand into their faces, which blinded them for several seconds.

That allowed Tanner the time he needed to recover from the shot he received, and he sent his fifth shell at the men. It struck one guard square in the chest, and he ceased to exist as anything other than a thousand chunks of meat and bone. Much of that bone ripped through the bodies of his comrades. Anyone not killed by the blast outright was laying on the sand, bleeding and moaning from multiple wounds.

Tanner rushed toward the house with one grenade left in the M32 and used it to blast his way into the home. The grenade created enough damage to cause a section of the second floor to collapse.

Tanner dropped the empty weapon and took out his

gun as he strode over the rubble and avoided the flames. Before venturing too far inside, Tanner slit open a waterproof pouch that was hanging at his side and removed the night vision monocular that was inside it. Tanner strapped the optics to his head but didn't activate it or flip down the monocular, as there was light visible in the hallway beyond.

Outside, the sun was making its inexorable progress and the night was ending, but if Tanner had to search for Adams in a dark place he wanted to be prepared.

With the night vision gear at the ready, Tanner ventured deeper into the house. When he heard footsteps on his right, he swiveled his gun that way, but saw an unarmed middle-aged woman wearing a nightgown and slippers.

The woman looked terrified and let out a scream. Tanner gestured for her to be quiet and to run out of the home the way he had entered.

The woman spoke to him in Greek, a language he didn't know, but he assumed she was either a housekeeper or a cook. Tanner gestured once more for the woman to leave. She did so, while never taking her eyes off the weapon he held.

Tanner then moved on to the staircase, where he detected two guards as he peered around a corner. They looked like sentries and were guarding access to the stairs and the second floor from their position on the landing. That told Tanner that Adams was still alive. No one guards a corpse.

Tanner ran toward the stairs while firing and wounded both guards in the legs. One of the men tumbled down the stairs, while the other returned fire, but his aim was so bad that he shot his partner in the side after the man had come to rest at the foot of the steps.

Tanner killed the guard who remained on the landing with a shot to the head and then realized that the guard who had fallen was out of the fight and had lost possession of his gun.

The weapon, a Beretta, lay on the floor of the landing. Tanner grabbed the fallen weapon and moved up the stairs. Time was growing short and he needed to kill Adams and make his escape.

As he reached the second floor, Tanner lowered the night vision monocular into place, as the second floor had lost power due to the fire. It was filling with smoke and thick with shadows. He heard a faint but distinct sound coming from outside and immediately knew what it was. It was a helicopter. Adams was planning on flying out of there.

The second floor hallway was dense with smoke, but beyond it, Adams' bedroom was engulfed in flames and the fire was spreading. There was the body of a guard lying just outside the room. The corpse had burns over most of it.

Tanner encountered no one else as he looked for access to the roof, while coughing from the smoke. He found the way to the roof in the form of a metal spiral staircase that led up to a closed metal door.

From outside came the faint sound of distant rifle fire, but it was brief. Still, he wondered if the boat Alexa was on had taken fire from someone in the helicopter.

Tanner ran up the steps. There was little time to do anything else that would be more cautious, as the sounds of the approaching helicopter grew louder.

The door was made of metal, but the lock looked flimsy. After removing the monocular, Tanner opened the door with a kick, and the sea breeze outside was refreshing after inhaling the smoke.

The first thing Tanner saw was the helicopter diving toward the roof, as if it had been approaching from a great height. Then, he saw Adams standing beside a guard who was dressed in a set of hooded coveralls and sunglasses. The guard held no weapon, but Adams was brandishing an AK47.

Tanner was taking aim at Adams when the hand appeared. It was the single biggest hand that Tanner had ever seen, and it engulfed his own hand, gun and all. Such was the force of the pressure the hand exerted, that Tanner was certain the bones in his fingers were breaking.

The man who owned the hand came into view. Tanner marveled at the size of him. He was a Greek who stood well over seven feet tall and had the musculature of a bodybuilder. The man used his other hand to punch Tanner in the face, just beneath the left eye. Afterwards, the man picked Tanner up and flung him toward the edge of the roof. Tanner hurtled through the air, went over the side, and plummeted toward the ground over thirty feet below.

16

DONE!

Alexa pointed toward the smoke rising from the island, as Sara became aware of the helicopter approaching from the east. The sleek aircraft looked as if it had flown right out of the newly risen sun and it was headed straight for the island.

"If Adams makes it onto that helicopter it will take some time to locate him again," Sara said. "I hope Tanner has already fulfilled the contract."

Alexa continued to stare at the smoke with worried eyes. "I just want Tanner to make it off that island in one piece. I wish he would have let me go with him."

"You wanted to join him?" Sara asked.

"Yes, but he said that he works alone."

"It's better this way," Sara said. "If you were over there he would be worried about you, and possibly distracted."

Alexa turned and glared at Sara. "That's how you see me, isn't it, as a distraction? Or maybe you see me as competition for Tanner's heart. Which is it?"

Sara laughed. "I have no romantic interest in Tanner, or any other man for that matter, but he is important to my plans. And yes, I think you're a distraction he doesn't need."

"Not everyone wants to be alone, Sara, and I won't do anything that would harm Tanner."

Sara was about to answer when the helicopter lowered its altitude and drew closer. After slowing its approach, it hovered a few hundred yards away and a rifleman appeared in an open doorway. The sniper got off a shot that just barely missed Alexa and drilled a hole into the side of the boat.

A second rifle boomed. It was Deke, who stood atop the cabin's roof. He was holding a .300 Winchester Magnum modified with a Jewell trigger, and which had a scope attached. His single shot blew apart the sniper's skull and sent his headless corpse tumbling from the chopper and into the water below.

Afterwards, Deke fired several shots at the chopper's tail rotor. That made the pilot of the helicopter climb and continue his path toward the island.

Alexa grinned at Deke. "Thank you. You saved my life."

Deke couldn't hear her. His ears were still ringing from the blast of the gun; however, he took her meaning and sent her a wink.

"Glad to help, beautiful."

Sara smiled at Deke and shouted up at him. "Maybe we should have hired you instead of Tanner."

Deke smiled back as he fed a fresh cartridge into the rifle. His hearing was clearing up and he could make out Sara's words.

"Our boy will get the job done. I don't think Tanner knows how to fail."

TANNER WAS HEADED TOWARD AN IMPACT WITH THE ground when he reached out a hand and snagged the edge of a stone planter. The planters had been built into the window sills on the second floor of the home but were all devoid of plants or flowers.

Tanner was able to keep his grip with his left hand, but the right hand was numb and soon slipped free. He had lost the gun to the giant that had tossed him off the roof, but still had his knife.

By the time he climbed back onto the roof, the chopper had landed, and he watched as the guard in the hooded jumpsuit clambered aboard. As Adams was about to climb onto the chopper with the AK-47 slung across his back, Tanner flung his knife and hit Adams in the side, which caused the man to scream out in agony.

Tanner had made the throw aiming for Adams' throat, but had to toss it with his left hand, because his right hand still felt numb. There was also a broken pinkie finger that was screaming with pain.

The man who had tossed Tanner over the side charged at him while bringing out a handgun. Tanner dived to his right and recovered his own gun from where it had landed, but the big man fired first.

His shot hit Tanner in the chest in the same spot on the body armor where he'd been struck earlier. The pain of the impact caused Tanner to shoot off target, and he caught the big man in the calf, causing the behemoth to stumble.

The giant held his arms out to regain his balance, but moved too close to the helicopter's tail blades, which sliced his gun hand off up to the wrist.

Blood flew everywhere, and Tanner felt some of the warm spray hit his face. The giant bellowed in shock and bewilderment as he looked at the bloody stump where his hand had been.

Tanner stood and rushed past the man, to shoot at Adams, who had just recovered from the initial agony of being wounded between the ribs. The bullet hit Adams' rifle, shattering the stock, and sending a piece of the damaged weapon into the side of Adams' neck. That caused Adams to gag, but the wound appeared to have done little damage, as it missed any major arteries.

As Tanner approached the chopper door, the pilot took off with only the guard in the coveralls aboard.

Tanner stared up at the guard, but couldn't see his eyes behind the dark glasses, while the hood obscured more of the man's face. Then, the chopper was in the air and headed back toward the mainland. It didn't matter to Tanner. He had Adams and that was all he needed.

The knife in the side had been excruciating for Adams, while the wound to the throat had been painful, but not life-threatening.

Adams was still alive and staring up at Tanner from where he was kneeling on his knees. He had his hands pressed to his throat in an effort to staunch the trickle of blood from his neck wound, which he probably thought was worse than it was.

Adams raised up a bloody hand and begged for mercy.

"Don't kill me. I'm not—"

Tanner's next bullet ended Adams plea for mercy.

When Tanner looked back at the giant, he saw that the man was flat on his back and breathing rapidly. He was in shock and dying from the massive blood loss caused by his severed hand and spurting wrist.

The sound of a motor came from the rear of the building. Tanner walked over to see a boat taking off from a small dock. The remaining guards had to assume that

Adams was dead or had flown off in the chopper. Either way, there was no one left to protect, and so the men were fleeing to safety.

Tanner counted only three of them, along with the woman wearing the robe he had seen earlier. He let them go. Adams was dead and if the rats wanted to flee a sinking ship then let them.

Tanner flexed his right hand and was certain that his pinkie was broken, while his left shoulder still ached after having borne most of the stress from stopping his fall. His left eye was swelling shut too, from the blow the giant had given him.

Before leaving the rooftop, Tanner took several pictures of Adams' corpse with a phone, then he went back through the house.

The second floor was like a furnace from the fire. Tanner held his breath and ran through the smoke and down to the ground floor. The home had a stone foundation but would be gutted by the flames without anyone fighting the blaze.

Tanner recovered Deke's M32 and found a portable marine radio inside the security office. He went outside and used it to call the boat. When Sara came on the mike, Tanner gave her the news.

"It's done."

17

LAZARUS

Tanner wore a splint on his broken finger.

His chest looked like one huge bruise and his left shoulder was sore. One eye was still swollen and turning black, but despite all the minor aches and pains, he felt good.

Adams was dead, the contract was fulfilled, and he was looking forward to more down time spent with Alexa.

By the afternoon, everyone had been awake for most of a day with scant rest, they decided to leave Greece as soon as possible and catch up on sleep while they flew back to Connecticut.

Tanner awoke aboard the jet to find that the sun had gone down, while Alexa was reclining beside him and still asleep. Deke and Garber were also asleep, but Sara was awake. She sent Tanner a smile as a way of greeting.

He moved across the aisle and sat beside Sara. "Have you talked to Burke?"

Sara nodded and then winced as she took in Tanner's black eye, which still had some swelling to it.

"You should have a doctor check out that eye."

"It's worse than it looks, and it's not the first time I've been punched in the face."

"Well, Mr. Burke was very pleased, as is the government. I would expect more offers in the future."

"I'll probably take the contracts, although I was surprised that Adams was so easy to kill."

"Easy? You nearly died in the attempt, and don't forget, you had to take two whacks at him because of that poor girl getting in your way. Maybe Adams was saved from other attempts on his life in the same fashion."

"That's a possibility," Tanner admitted. "But after surviving three other assassination attempts by trained killers, I'd have thought he'd be more of a challenge."

~

Hours later, they landed to find a limousine awaiting them. Everyone climbed into it except for Garber, whose wife was meeting him inside the terminal. Tanner thanked Garber for his help and then the limo was on the move.

It was late, and Sara, Tanner, and Alexa were headed to a hotel while Deke would be dropped off at his apartment.

"Why a hotel, Blake?" Tanner asked Sara. "Aren't you settled in here yet?"

"Not yet, and I travel so much that a hotel still makes sense for me, but I'll have to find an apartment soon."

"There are vacancies in my building," Deke said. "In fact, someone just moved out of the apartment that's below mine."

Sara asked Deke where he lived, then nodded with recognition when he told her.

"I know exactly where that is; one of my aunts lived in

OCCUPATION: DEATH

that building when I was younger. The rooms are huge. Have the owners kept the place up?"

"It was renovated two years ago. It's pricey because it's so close to the park, but it's also near the Burke corporate campus."

"I'll look into it," Sara said, while at the same time, her phone rang. Sara said hello and then listened as her eyes emitted worry. When she ended the call, Sara did so with a sigh and spoke to Tanner. "That was Mr. Burke. He's sending me a photo that he wants you to see. He said he would like you to explain it."

"What's that mean?" Tanner said.

"I don't know, but the man did not sound happy."

Sara looked back down at her phone and saw that she had received a new photo. When she opened it, she gasped in surprise and shook her head.

"It's not possible."

"What is it, Blake?"

Sara handed Tanner her phone and he stared at the photo.

It was a photo of Julien Adams. A new photo, and he was holding a copy of The Guardian, a London newspaper.

The paper had a current headline about an earthquake in California, a minor quake that had occurred while members of the British Royal Family had been visiting the state.

Beneath the headline titled, A PRINCE IN MORE THAN NAME, there was a photo showing the young prince reacting to the tremors by bravely shielding his wife with his body, as small bits of debris rained down on them from a ceiling. No one was injured, but that earthquake had occurred hours after Tanner had supposedly killed Adams.

If someone wasn't manufacturing fake photos for some reason, then that meant that Adams still lived. But how?

The phone chirped again. There was another photo. Tanner sent it to the screen and saw a second photo of Adams. He held no newspaper in the second photo.

Instead, he was grinning and giving the finger to the camera.

Adams was telling Tanner that he had not only failed, but that he could go fuck himself.

Tanner handed Sara back her phone.

"It looks like I'll have to kill the bastard again."

18

FAR ENOUGH

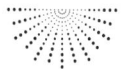

Tanner and Alexa arrived at the Burke corporate campus the following morning to find Sloane Lennox and Brad Grant standing outside on the curb, as if they had been awaiting their arrival.

There were also six armed security guards with Sloane, who spoke to Tanner while hiding behind them.

"Mr. Tanner, I see that Brad's assertion that you were a benefactor of unusually good fortune is proving to be true. It also appears as if your luck ran out in Greece. You failed Tanner. I'll not only get Conrad Burke to replace you on this project, but I'll also see to it that you return every dime we paid you."

Tanner didn't even bother to answer Lennox. He had spotted Sara standing near the building's entrance and walked over to join her.

Sara smiled in greeting. "Ignoring Lennox was the best way to handle him."

"The man is a joke," Tanner said.

Sara led Tanner and Alexa through a locked door that would avoid the metal detectors. The guard at the desk studied Tanner with interest, knowing that he was likely armed if he were being escorted through that door.

Sara sent the guard a nod and a wave and headed for a bank of elevators, while Tanner and Alexa followed.

Sara swiped a key card across a panel and one of two gold elevators opened. Tanner, Alexa, and Sara stepped aboard just as Lennox and his entourage approached. Brad Grant was about to step onto the elevator, but Tanner pushed him back.

"Get your own."

Grant's face twisted into a look of hate, and he pointed a finger at Tanner. "You and I are going to go head-to-head someday, Tanner."

Alexa smiled at Grant. "If that ever happened, it would be the last day of your life."

Grant's hateful gaze turned to stare at Alexa, but he said nothing more and the elevator doors closed.

Sara sighed. "I have to warn you. Mr. Burke is not happy this morning and he's leaning toward removing you from this project."

"What did you have to say about that?"

"I explained to him that regardless of what he decided, that you would kill Adams if it was the last thing you ever did."

"That's exactly right, Blake. I'm glad to see that someone here gets it."

"Oh, I understand you, Tanner, maybe even better than you know."

Tanner stared at Sara, but she was facing the doors and wore no expression. She was dressed in a conservative gray business suit with a skirt that hung down to the tops of her knees. Tanner thought the suit did little to disguise the curvy body beneath it.

Sara's raven hair gleamed beneath the fluorescent

lights of the elevator, her lips and nails shined with red gloss, and she wore a scent that Tanner found intoxicating.

Tanner's feelings for Sara once bordered on hatred. But while they spent time together in Guambi, his animosity toward her lessened, and he even found her pleasant to be around. Recently, she became his advocate, and because of their tumultuous past, each of them knew the other in ways that no one else did, which fostered mutual respect.

Looking at her in the elevator, Tanner wondered if they would ever put their past behind them where it belonged and come to trust each other. He hoped so, because despite their past, he liked her, although he would probably never admit it.

The elevator doors opened onto the outer office of Burke's CEO and a middle-age blonde introduced herself as Burke's executive assistant. Her name was Ella, and she escorted them into Burke's office.

As Tanner stepped inside, Burke stared at him with a harsh gaze, but waited to speak until after his assistant had closed the door upon her departure.

"I am not happy with your failure, Tanner."

"I can understand that, Burke, but it doesn't mean that I give a damn. I killed Adams on that rooftop in Greece, or at least I thought I had, but after thinking it over, I've an idea what actually happened."

Before Burke could ask Tanner to elaborate, Brad Grant entered the room followed by Lennox, the six guards, and an apologetic looking Ella. Burke pointed at the guards and told them to wait for Lennox in the outer office with his assistant.

Lennox protested, while gesturing toward Tanner. "We may need them to protect us from this animal here."

"They aren't cleared to listen to what we'll be

discussing, but Grant can stay."

Lennox didn't look pleased by the decision but accepted it and stood to the left of Burke's desk with Brad Grant standing in front of him like a human shield.

"I want Tanner dismissed, Conrad. The man is obviously incompetent."

"Be silent for a few moments, Sloane, Tanner has a theory I want to hear."

"I think that Adams is using doubles," Tanner said. "I killed one of them thinking he was Adams. The ex-Navy SEAL who reported that he shot Adams in the head was likely deceived the same way I was."

Burke nodded at that. "It would explain how the man is still alive, and perhaps he was never on that island at all."

"No," Tanner said. "He was there. I believe he was the man I saw the first time I attempted to kill him. The real Adams was the man who ran inside the safe room. I also think he was on that rooftop, although I didn't recognize him."

"Explain that statement," Burke said.

"The Adams I killed was holding a gun while the guard standing beside him was unarmed. I thought it odd at the time, but I was focused on killing the man I thought was Adams and didn't give it much concern. I was also fighting to stay alive myself."

A small smile appeared on Burke's lips. "That is a nasty shiner you have there. But this unarmed guard, did he resemble Adams at all?"

"Most of his face was hidden behind sunglasses and a hood. But if that was Adams, he got a good look at me."

The phone on Burke's desk buzzed softly while also blinking rapidly. Burke answered it and learned that he had an important call. He told his assistant to send it through and asked Tanner to hold on for a moment.

When Burke hung up after taking the call, he reached for a remote on the desk and activated the huge flat screen TV that took up most of the rear wall. Tanner, Sara, and Alexa stood and turned to see what Burke wanted to show them.

"I had someone take pictures of the man we believed was Adams. The pictures, video actually, was taken in the morgue in Greece, and it's enlightening."

Lennox spoke up, as a sour look crossed his distinguished face. "I do hope that this video isn't too graphic, Conrad."

"Relax, Sloane, you'll be able to keep your breakfast down. In fact, we'll only be looking at a lip."

"A lip?" Sara said, as one appeared on the screen. It was a close-up, and on the huge screen the lip was the size of a torso. Someone was pulling it down from the lower teeth of the corpse and it was plain to see the tattoo on the inner lip.

The tattoo read, #2.

Sara pointed at the screen.

"Tanner is right. Adams is using body doubles. I would bet that the man the Navy SEAL shot in the head had a tattoo on his lip as well, although with a different number."

Sloane waved a dismissive hand at the screen. "This is interesting but let us not forget that it doesn't change the fact that Tanner failed and failed miserably. Not only is Julien Adams still alive, but now we have no idea where he is, and it could take months to locate him."

Tanner walked over to Lennox, who cowered behind Grant.

"This is only a delay. I never fail, and I never fail because I never quit. I will kill Adams, if not today then soon, because I won't stop until he's dead."

Lennox looked away from Tanner's intense eyes and

spoke to Burke. "I say we fire Tanner and hire that Sicilian that Brad mentioned. From all accounts he's better than Tanner."

Alexa said, "No one is better than Tanner at killing. Bringing in someone else would only be a waste of time. Tanner will kill Adams."

"No one asked your opinion, young lady," Lennox said.

Sara leaned over Burke's desk to stare down at her boss. "Would you like my opinion? After all, this is my project."

Burke gestured for her to continue.

"Give me a week to locate Adams and let Tanner do what he was hired to do. This is simply a setback, nothing more and nothing less. Tanner will kill Julien Adams and I'm willing to stake my future in the company on that."

Burke stared up at Sara for several seconds, and then spoke. "We'll meet back here in a week and reevaluate, if it's needed. In the meantime, use whatever resources you require to locate Adams... the real Adams."

"I still think we should hedge our bets by bringing in that Sicilian," Lennox said.

"No, Sloane. Tanner is our man, and we'll stick with him. I trust that he and Miss Blake will get the job done. Now that's it, everyone leave. I've other work to do."

Lennox marched out in a huff with Brad Grant following, dismissed the other guards, and then entered a hallway to walk to his own office.

Sara, Tanner, and Alexa took the elevator down several flights to Sara's office. Her office was large and had a view of the lake at the center of the campus. She also had an assistant, a young Asian woman who looked Alexa over with interest while only glancing at Tanner.

"Mariah, please bring me everything we have on Julien Adams, both hard files and digital."

"Yes Sara. And is there anything else? Coffee maybe?"

"Coffee sounds good, bring a carafe and three cups."

After her assistant left, Sara spoke to Tanner. "I'll understand if you don't want to help in the search for Adams, since going through the files is likely a waste of time, but it's all I can think to do at the moment."

Tanner smiled. "I actually have a lot of experience tracking down a target by looking through files and paperwork. Being a hit man isn't all bang bang shoot 'em up."

"Sara?" Alexa said.

"Yes?"

"Is Deke here today? There's something I'd like to ask him."

"Um, yes, he's in his workshop inside the armory. Do you remember where it is?"

"I can find it."

"Hold on, you'll need a visitor's pass." Sara walked out to her assistant's desk where she grabbed a swipe card from a middle drawer and handed it to Alexa. "Use that to access the elevators, but Garber or Deke will need to let you into the armory."

Alexa thanked Sara and then kissed Tanner. "I'll be back soon."

"All right," Tanner said.

After Alexa left, Sara made an observation.

"You must have a relationship built on trust. Deke is a good looking guy."

"I don't own Alexa, and yes, I trust her."

"And do you trust me?"

Tanner smiled. "About as far as I could throw you."

Sara reached over and gave his biceps a squeeze.

"That might be far enough."

19

SHIP AHOY!

Deke smiled wide as he saw that his visitor was Alexa.

After letting her inside the armory, he led her back to where his workshop was, and they settled beside each other on an old black leather sofa.

"It's good to see you, Alexa. Is this visit one for business or just to shoot the breeze?"

"I just came to talk. It's not often that I find someone as interested in edged weapons as I am. Most people love their guns."

"Ain't that the truth, but I was a sword junkie growing up and took fencing lessons. Guns were never a big deal to me, since my family was in the business, but swords were cool, and I love a finely balanced knife."

They began talking about the exotic knives and swords that they had used and come across over the years, and the time flew.

At one point, Deke had to see to a matter that needed his attention, as Garber asked him to lend a hand with something. When he returned, he took out his phone and showed Alexa photos of his collection of bayonets.

"How old are those, Deke?"

"Most are from the American Civil War."

Deke brought up more photos, and Alexa laughed when she saw what looked like miniature bayonet blades.

"What are those?"

"They're also bayonets, and very old. My grandfather collected them. They were for pistols, believe it or not."

"You have quite a collection."

"This is nothing. There's a museum in Pennsylvania for edged weaponry. Whenever I go there I hate to leave."

"That sounds awesome, I'll have to go there someday."

"Alexa, what do you do for a living?"

"I had my own jewelry store for a time, but I sold it in order to get revenge on Alvarado."

"What's the story behind that, or is that too personal?"

"I'll tell you, but not here. Let's go get something to eat; I skipped breakfast."

"All right, and the cafeteria here isn't bad. They make a mean omelet."

As they were riding up in the elevator, Deke moved close to Alexa and asked a question.

"You and Tanner, that's serious?"

"Yes," Alexa said.

"That's what I thought. Brad Grant was right; Tanner is a lucky man."

~

Up in Sara's office, she and Tanner were looking through every photo they had of Julien Adams, as they searched for a lead to his whereabouts.

"Are you certain the man has no close ties to family or friends?" Tanner asked Sara.

"He was an only child whose mother was an orphan, and both his parents are now dead. There are cousins on his father's side of the family, but Adams never met them because they grew up in different areas of the country."

"What about friends, the man must have some?"

"All his so-called friends help him out for financial reasons. The government spread the word that Adams was doing something illegal, although they never formally accused him of aiding terrorists. If he ever had any real friends, he broke ties with them a long time ago."

Tanner picked up a photo of a yacht and stared at it. The ship was named the Sea Stalker. A younger Julien Adams was standing at the yacht's railing and staring down at the camera. It was an old publicity photo for an investor newsletter that Adams ran years earlier.

"I wonder if he still owns this boat," Tanner said, as he handed the photo to Sara.

"The records say that he sold it years ago, but... never mind."

"What were you going to say, Blake?"

"It's nothing, it's just that I saw a yacht in Rhodes, Greece that looked very much like this one. It had a similar name as well, it was called the Sea Beast."

"Can your assistant look into who owns that boat now, the one you saw?"

"Why? It's just a coincidence."

"It likely is, but it may also be something, and right now we need something. I will kill Adams, but I don't want to spend the rest of my life looking for him."

Sara had her assistant, Mariah, look up anything having to do with a yacht named the Sea Beast. Not knowing the ship's registry, her assistant came up with dozens of possibilities. Once they were sorted through by class and size, Mariah whittled the list down to three yachts, and she sent Sara everything she had been able to find concerning them.

By carefully comparing the photos of the three ships named the Sea Beast with Adams' Sea Stalker, they brought the list down to one, and that one looked like a perfect match.

"If it's not the same boat, I'd say that it's the exact same model," Sara said.

"They're the same, I'm sure of it," Tanner said, as he studied photos of the yachts beneath a magnifying glass. "There aren't many yachts of that size, and look at the design of the windows. Those are custom-made marine windows. Both yachts have the same type."

Sara took the magnifying glass from Tanner and studied the photos. The ships seemed the same to her, and she smiled as she looked over at Tanner.

"When I saw this boat, there was a man working aboard it that I recognized. His name is Cole McManus. When I knew him, he was a CIA agent, but the man working with him called him Shamus."

"Did he spot you?"

"No, but you realize what this means, don't you?"

Tanner nodded. "It means that Adams still owns this yacht. I'd also be willing to bet that this McManus is the mole in Adams' organization."

"Exactly."

"Where is the ship at now?"

"It's on a course for London and Adams was holding up a UK newspaper in the photo he sent us. He must have flown ahead, and his decision to flaunt the fact that he was still alive will come back to bite him in the ass."

"Good work, Blake."

"Thanks Tanner, but it was mostly luck, and now we have to cash in on it."

"Get that jet pointed toward London. It's Adams, *the real Adams*, time to die."

20

SMILES AND FROWNS

Sara asked Deke to join them on their trip to London. Tanner didn't object, as he had found the man to be an asset in his first attempt to kill Adams.

Deke said that he would be happy to come along, and Tanner didn't miss the smile on Alexa's face when Deke agreed to join them. While on the flight to London, Tanner asked Alexa about Deke.

"You like him a lot, don't you?"

She grinned at him. "Are you jealous?"

"No, but I am concerned. I would hate to lose you."

Alexa kissed Tanner, a long passionate kiss. When it ended, she stared into his eyes.

"I'm with you. Deke and I are just friends and he understands that."

"Good."

"What happens with us once this contract is fulfilled?" Alexa asked.

"What do you mean?"

"Well, we could go back to Hawaii, but I'm growing tired of hotels and want to settle down somewhere."

"You want to buy a house?"

"Yes, or rent, but where should we settle?"

"You mean live together?"

Alexa stared at him. "Am I assuming too much?"

Tanner kissed her. "No, we'll give it a go and see where it leads. I like being around you."

"It's mutual, so why don't we buy a house?"

Tanner gave a small shrug. "I've lived most of my life in various motels and hotels, but I'll settle wherever you want to live."

"I guess we'll try the east coast, since you might be working out of Burke for a while. But not a city. I want to live somewhere more… suburban."

Tanner laughed.

"What?" Alexa said.

"I was just imagining myself as a middle-class homeowner. I haven't used a lawnmower since I was a kid."

"I just want to live a calm life for a while. Can you understand that?"

"Yes, and I could use some normal in my life as well, but first, first I kill Adams."

~

While Tanner and Alexa were talking, Sara was speaking with Deke.

"I filled out an application for an apartment in your building before we left Connecticut, the woman who showed me around, Mrs. Kearns, she said that she would be in contact soon."

"Cool, we may be neighbors."

"Mrs. Kearns showed me the apartment that she said was right beneath yours, and I really like it."

Deke turned in his seat until he was facing Sara. "Are you seeing anyone, Sara?"

"Why? Are you asking me out on a date?"

"Hell yes, if you're available."

"I'm flattered, Deke, but I'm off the market. I've had such bad luck in the romance department that I've decided to stop dating, at least for now."

"Just my luck. I meet two incredible women and they're both unavailable."

"You're talking about Alexa, aren't you?"

"Yeah, but she only has eyes for Tanner. Is that why you two don't get along? Did Tanner get with her after you two dated?"

"Tanner and I were never together."

"No? But there's a history there, yes?"

"Yes, and it's complicated, but don't give up on Alexa forever. I think she likes you."

Deke blew out a sigh and leaned back in his seat. "This romantic shit is a pain in the ass."

"And the heart as well," Sara said.

⁓

THE JET LANDED AT HEATHROW AIRPORT. SARA, ALEXA, and Deke used their own names, but Tanner was traveling under the false identity of Richard Alban.

They were ferried by a limo to a hotel in the heart of the city. After unpacking in their respective rooms, they each showered and changed clothes. Afterwards, the limo delivered them to Burke's corporate headquarters in London, where they were met by a young woman named Candace Oliver. Oliver, who was a natural redhead, had an incredible body and dressed to show it off, as her skirt rode high and her neckline plunged to reveal a freckled cleavage.

After handing out thick envelopes that contained a small amount of currency in both pounds and euros, along with cell phones, Candace told Sara that she was there to assist her in any way she could. She then looked Tanner up and down and made an observation.

"Mr. Alban, you give the impression of being a ruffian with that black eye, and you're a handsome sexy devil, aren't you?"

"I see that not all Brits are staid, Miss Oliver," Tanner said.

"Call me Candace, and if you need anything, just ask and it's yours."

Alexa stepped forward. "I'll see to Mr. Alban's needs."

"Whatever you say, sweetie, but Mr. Alban, my number is in that mobile I gave you."

Deke held up his phone. "Do I have that number as well?"

Candace smiled at him. "Yes you do, big boy, and don't hesitate to use it. I love American men."

Deke grinned. "Expect a call."

After Candace Oliver exited the conference room, Alexa pointed at the door. "That woman is a shameless slut."

"You say that like it's a bad thing," Deke said, and Alexa frowned at him.

~

DEKE HAD TOLD CONRAD BURKE WHAT HE NEEDED, AND Burke arranged to have it waiting for him in London. The materials and weapons Deke requested were illegal, but so was contract murder.

Deke's workshop was located behind three locked doors in a corner of the building's lowest level, and only Deke knew the codes to open them once he reset the locks.

Tanner joined Deke in his workshop. while Alexa went off with Sara to speak to Candace about arranging discreet transportation for everyone while they were in the UK.

Deke flipped the lights on in his workshop and locked the door behind them after Tanner entered.

"They didn't give you much space, did they?" Tanner said.

The workshop was one room that was only about two-hundred square feet. It contained two tables, a refrigerator/freezer, a folding table and two chairs, along with a workbench that had matching vise grips attached at either end.

There were also several cartons, many of which were still sealed.

Deke nodded as he looked around the room. "It's small, but Burke didn't skimp on supplies. Most of those cartons contain gun parts and tools, but that white carton on the bench is the one I wanted you to see."

Deke led Tanner over to the workbench and unsealed the carton. Inside were several bundles that were about half the size of a brick and covered in thick plastic.

Beside the white carton was a smaller gray carton. Deke opened it and revealed small tubular devices with wires sticking from one end. Tanner knew what he was looking at.

"That's C-4 and a box of fuses."

"That's right," Deke said, while smiling. "Do you think you might find some use for them?"

Tanner smiled back at him. He liked Deke, and the man was handy to have around. They were physically similar as well, and the same height, although Deke was more muscular than Tanner.

"I'm certain we'll be using it, but I'm not sure how yet," Tanner said. "First we have to verify that Adams will be on that yacht soon."

"There's enough C-4 here to blow up that yacht twice, so once we know he's aboard, we have to wait until he goes out to sea and then set it off."

Deke's use of the word, "We", startled Tanner a bit, as he had primarily worked alone since becoming a Tanner. However, the Burke Corporation's assistance in the form of Sara, Deke, and Garber had been beyond valuable. Tanner had to admit to himself that it was nice to have allies.

"Let's go join the women," Tanner said. "We need to come up with a plan of action."

~

Sara was using a small conference room as an office. Tanner and Deke found it empty and decided to wait there for Sara and Alexa to return. While they waited, Deke told Tanner about his time in the Marines and revealed that he had worked as a mercenary after leaving the Marine Corps, and that he had been living in California.

"The money was good, but it seemed like all I ever did was protect dirtbags and drug smugglers. That's why I went to work for the Burke Corporation when the offer came in, and so far, it's been interesting. I hope you keep taking contracts for Burke."

"I might, but first I still have to kill Adams."

Sara and Alexa returned with coffee, along with the news that they had gotten cars for everyone but Alexa, who would ride with Tanner. The cars weren't new, but they were anonymous and could be discarded if the need arose.

Tanner took the keys from Sara and thought that the car was just one more perk that came with working with partners. Had he been on his own, he would have had to waste time stealing a car and then switch plates with another vehicle.

Deke looked over at Alexa. "Why didn't you get a car for yourself?"

Sara laughed. "You should have seen her as I took a car for a test drive. She was just sitting in the passenger seat, but being on the left side of the road seemed to freak her out."

Alexa shrugged. "I couldn't help it. It was weird. Every time Sara made a turn I felt as if we were headed into oncoming traffic. I'll be all right to drive in an emergency, but I won't do so unless I have to."

"We need a plan of attack, Blake," Tanner said, to bring the conversation back to the subject at hand.

Sara suggested that they all sit at the small round conference table and talk.

"The first thing I have to do is to contact Cole McManus. If he is the mole in Adams' organization, then he'll be invaluable."

"Did you two separate on good terms the last time you saw him?" Tanner asked.

Sara hesitated before answering, but then let the words out in a rush. "We were lovers and I dumped him. He took it hard at the time, but it was years ago."

"What do you mean when you say he took it hard? Was he violent?" Tanner said.

"No, but he didn't want to accept it. We were serious, that is, until I found out he was married. He left his wife when I dumped him so that we could be together, but I no longer trusted him, and so it ended, mostly."

"Mostly?" Alexa said.

"He stalked me, nothing too creepy, but he would sit in his car outside my apartment. He had an older partner that he respected, and the man talked some sense into him. After that, we ran into each other twice. I was working exclusively on my career and he was back with his wife, who was pregnant. We ended as friends. This all happened years ago when I was still a rookie agent."

Tanner leaned back in his seat.

"Do you think he'll be willing to help?"

"I do, as I said, despite everything, we ended as friends."

"Are you certain that he's still with the CIA?" Tanner asked.

"I have no way to verify that, but he must be if he's really the mole we think he is, and he is using an alias."

"How soon can you make contact?"

"Tonight. If he's on that yacht, they'll be docking soon. I'll contact him when he leaves it, after days at sea, the crew will want some time to relax in the city."

"Carry a gun, Blake, just in case."

"Are you worried for my safety, Tanner?"

"Not really, I know better than anyone that you're hard to kill."

"I could say the same about you."

Tanner and Sara smiled at each other, while sitting between them, Alexa frowned.

21

THE LIES WE TELL OURSELVES

Sara contacted Cole McManus while the man was having a pint with his mates from the Sea Beast inside a pub near the dock.

McManus looked surprised, and then alarmed, when he spotted Sara sitting at the bar, as he feared she might blow his cover. However, Sara sent him a smile and made no move to join him at his table.

McManus walked to the bar and looked her over. "Good God, Sara, you're even more beautiful than I remember."

"Thank you," Sara said, as she stared back at McManus, who was ten years her senior. McManus was blond, muscular, and handsome, although he displayed signs of being a heavy drinker. There were also laugh lines upon his face that hadn't been present when Sara had known him well years ago.

They had become lovers when she was still somewhat naïve, and he had been her first love as an adult. After it ended badly, Sara threw herself into her work and didn't become involved with anyone until she'd met Brian Ames.

Given that the three most intense romantic relationships in her life all ended badly, and even tragically, Sara's decision to remain alone seemed her best choice, although she did feel lonely at times.

McManus leaned closer and whispered. "I'm working undercover and going by the name of Shamus Breen."

"You're also working as a mole in Julien Adams' organization," Sara whispered in return, and watched as Cole's eyes widened in alarm.

"We're leaving," Cole said, and he took Sara by the arm and headed for the door. As they passed the table where his friends sat, Cole sent them a wink. "Me and the lass are going somewhere to talk in private, boys. I'll see you all in the morning."

He received winks in return, along with wolf whistles of appreciation directed at Sara, and then they were out on the street.

"I'm not here to hurt you, Cole," Sara said.

"Do you have a car?" Cole asked.

Sara answered by taking out her key fob and unlocking her car, which caused the vehicle's lights to blink. Cole moved toward it while still gripping Sara's arm. She was annoyed by the rough treatment, but didn't try to break free of his grip, as she hadn't wanted to cause a scene that would bring attention to them.

Once inside the car, Cole held up a finger and spoke through gritted teeth. "What the fuck are you up to? I know you're no longer with the Bureau."

"I'm with the Burke Corporation, Cole. I'm the one running the Adams operation."

"Really?" Cole said, as his anger dissipated. "All right, you're with Burke, but that still doesn't explain how you knew where to find me. And don't try to give me any shit about this being just a coincidence."

"No, I'm making contact with you because while searching for Adams I stumbled across the fact that you're the mole in his organization."

"How did that happen?"

"I saw you aboard the yacht in Greece, and later realized that the boat was connected to Julien Adams."

Cole gasped and then smiled. "The attempts on Adams' life on the island, that was Burke's assassin?"

"It was."

McManus laughed. "My people told me that Adams was blaming a man named Omar Ali Rashid, because Rashid was the only one who knew that Adams was living on that island. And your asset failed, you know? Adams is still alive, but I don't know where he is now."

"He's on that yacht, or he soon will be, that's our guess."

Cole rubbed his chin as he thought that over. "Yeah, it makes sense. They use me and another man to ferry the yacht around, but they always give us some time off when Adams is due aboard, and we're not to report back tonight. My guess is that they're securing the boat by checking for listening devices, bombs, that sort of thing."

"Have you ever been near Adams?"

"Hell yeah, several times aboard the yacht."

"If you've been in such close contact with the man then why haven't you killed him yourself?"

Cole's eyes flashed with anger. "It would be suicidal to try to kill the man on that yacht. He's protected at all times and doesn't even leave the stateroom until we're at sea. Besides, I'm kept pretty busy with my work aboard the vessel. It was luck that I was able to get this close at all."

"The man is using body doubles; we've confirmed it."

"That explains why that former Navy SEAL, Cameron Bonds, said he had blown Adams head off. I nearly fainted when I saw the man walking around fine the next day, and then I was unable to get in contact with Bonds again."

"Our man killed another of the doubles and now he's here to kill the real Adams. I need you to let us know when he boards that boat."

"The man may not even come on board. Adams owns more than one yacht, although, I've never been on the others. From what you say, he may send a body double as a decoy."

"I still need you to let me know if Adams or a double comes aboard."

"I can't. I have no way of knowing, and besides, once I'm back on that yacht, we'll be setting sail for parts unknown."

Sara let out a sigh. "Why are you undercover as a deck hand? You would have been better placed as a bodyguard."

"Tell me about it. That was what we tried to do, but the guards are all hand-picked by a man named Suernos over in France. He runs mercs, used to be one himself and he doesn't use anyone that he doesn't know or that one of his men can't vouch for."

"This Suernos, what's his first name?"

"Who knows, Sara, you know how that works. Some guys just use one name, and no one knows who he really is, no one but the people he's close to."

Sara thought of Tanner and the fact that, despite studying and tracking the man for over a year, she still had no idea who he really was. But Alexa knew Tanner's true name, and that bugged Sara. In fact, it pissed her off.

"What's wrong?" Cole asked her. "You looked angry suddenly."

"It's nothing. But listen, our man not only killed one of Adams' doubles, he also killed a number of bodyguards.

Does that mean that Adams will be looking to replace them before leaving on his trip, or will he be understaffed with protection?"

"I have no way of knowing, but if he's getting new bodyguards, that probably means that Adams is in Paris, or nearby."

"We have to get him, Cole."

"Tell me about it. I've been playing Shamus Breen the deck hand for months. I'm sick of it and I just want to get back to New York City."

"Back to your wife?"

"No Sara, we divorced. She finally wised up and dumped me. But what about you? I heard about your meltdown and that you were kicked out of the Bureau, but what's going on in your personal life?"

"Work, Cole, just work, and that's how I like it."

Cole raised up his hands. "Chill, I wasn't coming on to you. That said, if you change your mind, I'm willing, and there will be no strings attached. I always liked you Sara, you know that."

"I do, and will you help me, Cole?"

"I'll do what I can, which isn't much. My people are opposed to killing Adams. They think the man would be more valuable as a snitch. My passing on information about the man is just their way of gaining favor with the agency that contracted with Burke."

"Would you wear a tracking device? We could give you one. If we know where you are, we'll know where Adams is too."

"I do most of my work in just a pair of shorts and deck shoes, besides, there is monitoring equipment on board, I've seen it, and no one is allowed a phone or access to the internet except Adams."

"I see, but you're willing to help if you can?"

"Of course, but I'll have to go through my superiors and tell them that you know who I am. If they don't yank me, I'll do what I can."

"Good. I'll tell Mr. Burke to give his contacts assurances that you won't be compromised. Once my asset kills Adams, we'll both be free to move on to other projects."

Cole sighed. "You're like me, aren't you? Work is all you have?"

"Yes, and it's enough for now."

Cole smiled bitterly.

"I tell myself the same lie."

22

PREPARATIONS

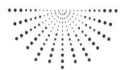

The following morning, Sara filled Tanner in about her meeting with Cole McManus, while Deke and Alexa joined them for coffee in the conference room at the Burke UK Headquarters.

"Is he going to be of any use?" Tanner asked. "It sounds like he's just an observer."

"Cole's superiors approved his involvement, although they think it's risky. Like you, I'm not sure what he could do to help. It sounds as if he has little freedom aboard that yacht. Adams' security routinely checks for wires and transmitters. Still, Cole is willing to help in any way he can."

"This Cole McManus told you that Adams has access to more than one yacht, but we have no way of knowing what the others are. He might also not be traveling by yacht at all," Tanner said.

Sara shrugged. "That yacht is our only lead; we have to hope that it pays off."

"I need to sneak aboard that yacht. I can use a Seabob to reach it if it drops anchor somewhere."

"That's no good, Tanner. Cole says that Adams will be heavily guarded, even if you got aboard, leaving alive is another story, and you'll be somewhere in the middle of the Atlantic Ocean."

Tanner nodded thoughtfully. "That Navy SEAL that drowned, Adams had him thrown overboard, he would likely do the same thing to me if he caught me."

"Maybe, or he might just have you shot," Alexa said.

Tanner looked thoughtful again, and then spoke to Deke. "The C-4, I may have a use for it, but I'll need your help."

"What are you thinking?" Sara asked.

"A back-up plan, or more of a doomsday device. If Adams killed me before I could get to him, the C-4 could ensure that I didn't fail."

Alexa reached over and took his hand. "I'd rather you'd be a living failure than a dead success."

"I'm not planning to fail or die, but I think I know how to kill Adams and still make it off that boat." Tanner stood. "Deke, let's go to that workroom of yours, we've a bomb to make."

~

Tanner and Deke made their bomb as Sara and Alexa watched. When it was done, Sara smiled with approval as Tanner told her his plan.

"It's risky, Tanner, but it should work. Still, it's dependent on a lot of things going just right."

"True, but if Adams is on another vessel besides that yacht, this bomb won't be used at all."

"Just make sure you aren't nearby when it goes off," Sara said.

"I won't be, Blake, at least not too close."

Deke had been wiping his workbench clean with a rag when something occurred to him and he leaned back against the bench and became lost in thought. As Sara and Tanner discussed contingency plans, Alexa walked over to speak to Deke.

"Deke? Are you in there?" Alexa said, while waving a hand in front of him.

Deke snapped out of the trance he was in and smiled at Alexa. "Sorry, I was just thinking of something that might help your boyfriend if he finds himself tossed off that yacht."

"What is it?"

"A breathing apparatus, a miniature one. Garber told me that he once rigged one in the heel of a boot that contained ten minutes of compressed oxygen. It was real James Bond stuff."

"I don't think there's enough time to get it here. Could you make one?"

"No, I don't have the equipment or know-how."

"That's okay, it's still nice that you're looking out for Tanner, and he likes you too, which I think is a rare thing."

"Yeah, he doesn't strike me as a guy who would have a lot of close friends."

"And what about you?"

"A few, guys I served with, but they're all scattered around the country, while one or two of them are still in the Marine Corps."

"Sara said you had worked as a mercenary. I can't see you as a hired gun. You have too much integrity."

"You barely know me, Alexa. Maybe I'm really a selfish bastard who will do anything to get what he wants."

"No. I know what you're like. I'm very good at reading people."

Deke stared at her. "Sara said that you were psychic. Is that true?"

"Yes."

Deke smiled as he looked her over. "What am I thinking now?"

Alexa laughed. "I don't have to be psychic to guess that, and speaking of that, have you made that call to Candace?"

"I did, and we had a very nice evening together."

"You saw the sights?"

Deke smiled. "It was a sight, yes."

"You slept with her?"

"A gentleman never tells," Deke said primly, and then he and Alexa both laughed.

Tanner cleared his throat as he walked over with Sara. "Am I interrupting something?"

"Deke was just telling me about his date with the lovely Candace."

"I wouldn't mind hearing the details of that myself," Tanner said, "But some other time. Right now, I want to go over the intricacies of our bomb again. I wouldn't want to activate it prematurely."

Deke walked over to where the bomb lay. "I can refine the trigger. I could even add voice activation, but there's too big a risk of it going off accidentally. The voice activation software is far from perfect."

"We'll stick with the physical triggers, but I want to make a change to the timer."

"You're still thinking of boarding that yacht while it's out at sea, aren't you?" Sara asked.

"I am, but I'll need McManus's help to do it. He'll have to lower a line over the side once it's at anchor, otherwise, I'll have no way to climb aboard."

"I'll contact Cole again tonight and finalize our plans."

"Are you certain he's not being watched?" Tanner asked.

"If he is it won't matter; we're meeting at a bar and then heading to a motel. Anyone watching will think we're having sex, not planning a hit."

"This McManus is a former lover of yours, so he might want to do both," Tanner said, and a slight smile was playing on his lips.

Sara smiled back at him. "Then he'll be out of luck."

Tanner looked her over. "His loss."

23

CAPTURED AS BAIT

That night, while Sara met with McManus, Tanner decided to show Alexa around London.

He had lived there for several weeks while a younger man and was surprised by how many changes London's East End had gone through. Most of it was due to the former Olympic Games that were held in the area, but the changes were still taking place.

Many warehouses were being converted into loft apartments while several trendy bars and cafes had sprouted up. Tanner and Alexa were enjoying one such bar that had a live local band when Alexa left Tanner at their table to use the ladies room, which was located at the end of a hallway and near a rear exit door.

On her way there, Alexa spotted a large Middle-Eastern looking man passing a wad of bills to a young white man in a suit who she thought might be the bar's owner or manager.

It had nothing to do with her, and she decided it was some sort of low-level graft. Perhaps the bar manager was taking a bribe to let the man peddle a cheaper brand of whiskey, or for the opportunity to run a string of hookers into the bar to pick-up customers.

Alexa had witnessed much corruption during her young life, having grown up in Mexico and being around the drug cartels. She knew that no country was immune to having its share of crime.

Two women left the bathroom soon after Alexa had entered, while another one took the stall next to hers after she had sat down. The woman left her stall when Alexa stopped at the sink to wash her hands. The woman stood beside Alexa and seemed to be checking her make-up in the mirror. Alexa guessed that the short woman was a local, judging by her manner and way of dressing, despite her dusky skin tone. When she spoke, and revealed a British accent, Alexa knew she had assumed correctly.

"Are you here with your boyfriend, luv?" the woman asked.

"Yes, he's showing me around London."

"Ah, he travels a lot, does he?"

"Yes, for business," Alexa said.

"And did he have some business in Boston a few nights ago," the woman asked, as she turned toward Alexa.

Alexa tensed, then swiveled about as the door opened and the Middle-Eastern man was standing there holding a gun.

Alexa was about to reach for the blades she carried, which were hidden in her hair. She was too late though, and the woman sprayed her in the face with something that took her breath away, while weakening her knees. By the time she collapsed to the bathroom floor, Alexa was barely conscious.

OCCUPATION: DEATH

Sara joined Cole McManus at the same pub where they had met the night before. After sharing a drink, McManus ordered a bottle to go. When they departed the bar, they did so to more winks and cheers from McManus's half-drunk friends.

"All those men don't work on Adams' yacht, do they?" Sara asked.

"No, just one other man, he's a cook, while the rest of them are guys who maintain the other vessels. Sara, I've been playing Shamus Breen for so long that I know the names of some of those guys' wives and children. This hit man of yours, this Tanner, he has to come through and kill Adams. If I have to keep cleaning toilets on that yacht, I'll go mad."

Sara stopped walking and stared at McManus. "How did you know that the asset's name is Tanner? I never told you his name."

"My boss told it to me. The CIA isn't the agency that decided to outsource the wet work to your people, but we have fingers in every other agency and know what's going on."

They reached the motel, which Sara found to be seedy, and soon they were in a small room that had a sagging bed, an ancient dresser, and a filthy bathroom.

McManus gestured around. "As you may remember, I would take you somewhere nicer than this to... meet, but lowly deck hand Shamus Breen can't afford better than this."

"It doesn't matter, we'll only be talking," Sara said.

McManus moved closer and cupped her face in his hands. "I was hoping that we might relive old times."

Sara stepped backwards, and McManus's hands fell away.

"I'm here to discuss business, that's all, Cole."

McManus shrugged and smiled. "You can't blame me for trying."

Sara sighed. "Back to business. We'll be tracking that yacht from a distance after it leaves the harbor. Do you have any idea where it might be headed, or when it will leave?"

"Actually, I do. I was told we'd be shoving off tomorrow, but I don't know what time. Meanwhile, I caught a glimpse of the charts the captain was looking over. It seems we're headed to the east coast of America."

"Really? That sounds like quite a trip."

"It is; the damn yacht only does about thirty knots at top speed, or say about thirty-five miles an hour."

"What about the other boats Adams has, were you able to learn the names of them?"

"No Sara, and I've been trying to do that long before you came along. The fact is, we still don't know if Adams will even be on the yacht. And if I spot him, will it be him, or one of his doubles? The man didn't stay alive this long by being stupid, you know?"

"I do, but I need this hit to go down. My reputation is on the line."

"If Tanner is anywhere near as good as I've heard, Adams will die, it's just a question of when."

Sara seemed to relax after hearing McManus words. "Tanner is the best. This will all work out."

"You still haven't told me the details."

"Tanner will be bringing a bomb aboard the yacht."

"A bomb? And just how am I supposed to survive the blast?"

"Once Tanner is aboard, he'll set the timers on the fuses and then the two of you will use a Seabob to gain distance from the yacht. You're still a strong swimmer, aren't you?"

"Hell yeah, and I've even used a Seabob before, but what sort of bomb are we talking about? Why would it need more than one fuse?"

"C-4, Tanner will actually be wearing it. Our gunsmith is replacing the metal plates of a bulletproof vest with C-4. Tanner will insert the fuses once he's aboard the yacht."

"That would work, but again, I'll have no way of knowing if Adams is aboard until we're underway and out at sea."

"I understand. That's why we'll need you to signal us."

"How?"

"Smoke would be best, perhaps a small fire?"

McManus sat on the bed and patted the spot next to him. "Come sit. I promise not to bite."

Sara sat beside McManus and he began to tell her about his life since they had known each other years ago. She remembered that McManus had been a rising star in the CIA, but now they had him taking undercover roles as a deck hand and he seemed to be ineffective.

There was also the divorce from his wife, a young daughter he never saw, and no life outside the Agency. Sara suspected that the man also tended to drink heavily, as there were prominent veins visible on his nose, and she had seen him down several beers in quick succession when she had first come across him in the pub the night before.

Her own bright career in the FBI had ended when she let her obsession with Tanner destroy her. Now, she had tied herself to the man as a way to rise in a new arena. The irony of it all made her chuckle, and McManus asked her what was so funny.

"My life is a mess," Sara said.

McManus screwed the top off the bottle of cheap wine he carried and handed it to her, but not until he had downed nearly half of it in a series of gulps.

"You're in good company, Sara."

Sara took the bottle and swallowed a mouthful. The cheap wine tasted like varnish.

McManus leaned over and kissed her. "Remember how good we were together, Sara? Don't you want to feel that again, if only for one night?"

Sara became tempted by the desire to do anything that would bring a moment of pleasure into her life and make the emptiness inside her go away. Still, she pushed McManus back and stood up, then handed him his bottle.

"Tanner will approach the boat from starboard, so you'll have to lower a line over on that side. And as I said, start a small fire in the galley if you can. It will act as a diversion and the smoke will be Tanner's signal that the line has been dropped and that Adams is on that yacht."

McManus nodded in agreement but said nothing.

Before opening the door to leave, Sara looked back at him. "Good luck, Cole, and perhaps I'll see you tomorrow."

McManus nodded again and then took a long swig from the bottle.

Sara walked out into the nightlife of London, as thoughts of the past swirled through her mind.

24

TURNABOUT IS FOUL PLAY

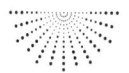

Tanner was wondering what was taking Alexa so long to return from the restroom, when the woman who had drugged Alexa sat across from him at his table. Tanner's black eye was fading, but still plainly visible, and the woman smiled as she took it in.

"I see that someone has hurt you. That means that my employer is not the only man who wishes you harm."

"Your employer? What's this about?"

The woman slid a phone across the table that had a picture of a drugged Alexa being held up by a large man who looked like an Arab. Tanner recognized the man. He had seen him standing at the bar earlier.

"What do you want?"

The woman smiled. "I want you to follow me on foot to a nearby building. If you refuse or cause me harm, the woman will be killed."

"How do I know she's not dead already?"

The woman sighed, made a short whispered call on her phone, and then passed it over to Tanner.

"You'll be getting a live feed soon. Do you know how to bring that up on that mobile?"

"I do," Tanner said, and then he asked the woman her name.

"You can just call me Jane, as in Jane Doe," the woman said, and there was a bit of Cockney accent in her tone.

Tanner leaned closer to her. "If you would like to keep living, Jane, you'll tell me where I can find my friend and then disappear."

"That sounds like a threat, Mr. Tanner. I may ask my friend to break one of the woman's arms."

Tanner said nothing more, but he brought up the live feed when the phone chirped. The man from the picture was holding up a laptop and his face filled the screen. When the man swung it to the right, Tanner saw a tearful Alexa sitting in an office chair inside what appeared to be a warehouse.

Alexa cowered when the man moved toward her, and Tanner had to stop himself from smiling. Alexa was playing the role of a helpless female, something she most definitely was not. The man with her hadn't even bothered to restrain her. Tanner was glad to see that Alexa was thinking on her feet.

"Talk to him," the man told her, and after sniffling, Alexa spoke into the camera.

"Baby, please do what they say? This man is huge, and I think they're waiting for someone else to arrive."

"Are you all right?"

"I feel okay. Whatever they drugged me with wore off, but oh, I'm so scared."

The man yanked the laptop back. Once again, his face loomed large on the screen. "Follow the woman who gave you the phone. If you hurt her in any way, I will kill this bitch of yours. Do you understand me?"

"I do," Tanner said.

"If you're armed, pass your weapon to the woman, carefully. We wouldn't want this to end in a tragedy."

Tanner took out the small pistol he'd been carrying in a pocket holster and passed it beneath the table to "Jane." She placed it in her purse.

He also had a knife hidden down the inside of his right boot, but decided to hold on to it.

"What's this about?" Tanner asked the man, but the screen on the phone went dead.

"Give me back my mobile, along with your own, and follow me out of here," the woman said.

Tanner did so, and they walked in silence for three blocks, before turning down an alley. There was a limousine parked at the alley's end, along with a small moving truck. Tanner knew that whoever was behind this was inside that limo. He wondered if Julien Adams had somehow tracked him down. After following the woman into a warehouse through a side door, he saw the big man from the bar, and Alexa.

The man asked the woman if Tanner had given her a gun, and when she produced it from her purse, he told her to point it at Tanner while he frisked him.

It was a bad frisk and it missed the knife in his boot. That would come back to haunt the man if Tanner had his way.

When Tanner moved toward Alexa, she jumped up and hugged him as if she were a frightened child and he was her father.

Alexa whispered in his ear. "What is this?"

"I don't know."

"I have two throwing knives; I'll make a move when you say the word, 'hungry', agreed?"

Tanner whispered yes and let her know about the knife

in his boot, then he held her at arm's length and checked her for injuries. There were none, other than a set of red eyes from the drug sprayed in her face, and the manufactured tears.

Alexa was so beautiful. She was also very deadly. Tanner thought that in some ways she was a mirror image of himself.

"Did he hurt you?" Tanner said aloud.

"He was mean and grabbed my arm roughly, but no, he didn't do anything too bad."

Alexa sniffled after saying that, then looked over at the big man and quickly away. She wanted the man and the woman to think she was terrified and not a threat. That way, they would never see her coming.

On the left, a corrugated metal door began to rise. When it opened fully, two men in work clothes wheeled in a portable toilet that was on a moving dolly. Whatever was sloshing around inside the tall green plastic box was some of the vilest human waste that Tanner had ever smelled, and standing beside him, Alexa gagged.

In a flash, Tanner understood what was going on, and had it confirmed when Omar Ali Rashid walked in. Tanner had dunked Rashid's head inside a portable toilet in Boston and the man wanted to return the favor.

The roll-up door went down, and Rashid smiled at Tanner. "We meet again, Mr. Tanner, and now it's time to turn the tables."

Tanner stepped away from Alexa while blocking the view of her from the man and the woman who had brought them there, and who were both aiming guns at them. He then sent a cold smile Rashid's way while pointing at the portable toilet.

"I'm going to make you eat whatever is inside that shitter, Rashid, so I hope you're hungry."

Behind him, Alexa freed the hidden throwing knives from her hair as Tanner charged toward Rashid, and all hell broke loose inside a London warehouse.

25
A PROMISE IS A PROMISE

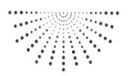

After trying to reach either Tanner or Alexa by phone and failing to do so, Sara received a call on her own phone. She was worried when she saw that it was from Conrad Burke. The only reason she could think of for Burke calling was to deliver bad news, such as informing her that he'd decided to cut Tanner from the project.

"Hello, Mr. Burke."

"Miss Blake, can you talk in private?"

Sara was climbing into her car when the call came in, and she shut the door.

"I can talk, sir."

"I need to contact Tanner. Do you know where he is?"

"No, and I've been trying to reach him as well. Is something wrong?"

"I have disturbing news. It seems that Omar Ali Rashid is in London, and I've reason to believe that he's out to get even with Tanner."

"How is that possible?"

"Brad Grant contacted Rashid and told him who Tanner was and where to find him."

"If that's true, then he was working for Sloane Lennox," Sara said, and there was anger in her voice.

"Miss Blake, it was Sloane who informed me of what Brad had done. He uncovered the fact that Brad had been looking through computer files that he shouldn't have been, and an investigation uncovered the truth. Unfortunately, Sloane confronted Brad before consulting me, and Brad left the building and hasn't been seen since."

"You're saying that he's in the wind?"

"Yes, and due to the sensitive nature of this, I can't exactly ask the police to look for him, and the man is well-liked among my own security force. However, I will be hiring outside help to locate him."

"I'll find him when I return to the states."

"If you want to handle this, you have my blessing."

"What about Sloane Lennox, sir, do you really believe he's innocent in this? You know how he feels about Tanner."

"Sloane has a strong opinion about Tanner, but I don't think he would wish the man dead, nor would he blatantly endanger the project."

"All right, and I'll let you know when I hear from Tanner."

"You don't sound very worried about him."

"I'm not. But if Omar Ali Rashid is after revenge on Tanner, you can be certain of one thing."

"What's that?"

"That Omar Ali Rashid is now a dead man."

"That will open up a can of worms, but it's Rashid's own fault. Good luck there, Miss. Blake."

"Thank you, sir, and if everything goes well, Julien Adams will be dead tomorrow."

A chuckle came over the line. "Miss Blake, things never

go the way we think they will, just make sure that you succeed. That's all that matters."

"Yes sir," Sara said, and then the line went dead.

∾

Alexa let out a soft grunt as she tossed her throwing knives at the woman known as Jane and the woman's huge accomplice.

The knives had pink handles, and when they were in her hair they appeared to be barrettes. They weren't barrettes, but finely balanced knives that Alexa had practiced with for many years.

The big man received a two-inch long knife blade to his left eye, while the woman fared a little better. Alexa's throw had embedded the knife in the woman's right cheek, spearing her tongue. The man was incapacitated by the knife in his eye, but the woman, although injured, recovered quickly and raised her gun to shoot at Alexa, who was now unarmed.

∾

Tanner rushed at Rashid even as Alexa let loose with her knives. The two men who had brought the portable toilet inside were local toughs wielding weighted batons. They raised them high as Tanner approached, even as Rashid stood frozen in place.

Rashid had expected Tanner to beg for his life, or to plead with him to spare the life of the woman he seemed to care for, but the man was attacking him just seconds after being threatened. Rashid was stunned by his brashness.

When he was a few feet away from Rashid, Tanner

leapt up, used the pudgy man as a brace while grabbing onto his shoulders, and slammed his feet into the chests of the pair with the batons.

All four of them collapsed to the floor of the warehouse, and as he fell, Tanner reached for the knife in his boot.

~

ALEXA GAVE THE CHAIR THAT SHE HAD BEEN SITTING IN a hard kick. It zipped across the concrete floor of the warehouse and slammed into Jane's knees.

It struck with enough force to throw off Jane's aim and her first shot missed Alexa by a foot. The second shot went into the ceiling, as Alexa had rushed the woman and grabbed her wrist with one hand, while twisting the knife in Jane's cheek with the other.

Jane shrieked in pain, just as her one-eyed partner took aim at Alexa's back. Before the man could fire, Tanner's knife entered his throat, severing an artery, and the gun dropped from the man's hand.

~

AFTER TOSSING HIS KNIFE INTO THE BIG MAN'S THROAT, Tanner spun around and ripped a baton from the grip of one of the men who had brought in the portable toilet.

The man said, "Hey!" a moment before Tanner brought the ball shaped end of the baton crashing down on the side of his partner's head. There was a sickening crunch heard, as the thug's skull cracked, and the man reached for the other baton, which his partner had just dropped.

He was able to grab it but let go as Tanner broke his

wrist with a vicious blow, and then followed it with one to his chin.

Two more blows assured that the man stayed down, but then Tanner lost his grip on the baton. He had only been able to clasp it with four fingers, as his pinkie was encased in a splint.

The blows had been enough, both men were out of the fight, while one appeared to be dead.

After reclaiming the baton from the floor, Tanner turned his attention on Rashid. Rashid had made it to his feet and was reaching into his pocket, possibly for a weapon. Tanner whipped the baton back and prepared to strike Rashid.

~

It wasn't a weapon Rashid was reaching for, but a phone, as Rashid had handled most of life's problems by calling someone else to deal with any difficulties that came his way.

As a boy, he called on his families' servants, then later, there were lawyers, or his esteemed brother. He had left his brother out of his trouble with Tanner, and for once in his pampered life, Rashid had decided to handle things himself.

Of course, handling things himself didn't mean he would actually do things himself. He had hired help to assist him, and he so wanted to make Tanner beg for mercy. His goal had been to disgrace the man the same way he himself had been debased and violated, by being dunked in filth.

With Tanner put in his place, Rashid would then order Tanner's death, but only after making the man watch his woman die. The people helping him would perform those acts gladly, as they had been paid handsomely to do so.

However, his helpers were being destroyed by Tanner and Alexa, and so Rashid reverted to type and reached for his phone to call his brother. Unfortunately for Rashid, no one could help him now.

∼

Tanner slammed the baton against Rashid's pocket with a succession of three quick swings that were no more than a blur. Rashid whimpered in pain, withdrew his hand from the pocket, and sobbed as he looked at his fingers, two of which were mangled and bleeding.

A thud sounded from behind, and Tanner turned to see the woman named Jane writhing on the floor with a gashed throat. The big man was on the floor at her side, with his own throat bleeding freely from the wound where Tanner's knife stuck out.

As Alexa walked over to join Tanner, while holding two guns, Tanner turned and smashed Rashid in the face with the baton.

The blow destroyed the man's mouth, and Rashid fell to his knees and spat out bits of broken teeth, along with gobs of blood.

Tanner caressed Alexa's cheek as he spoke to her. "Watch outside for any signs of police. This is London, and the sound of gunshots are rare. They'll be reported."

Alexa nodded and looked down at Rashid. "What are you going to do to him?"

"Something I promised him I'd do back in Boston. Apparently, he didn't take me seriously."

"Or me," Alexa said.

Tanner grinned. "That was their biggest mistake."

Alexa handed Tanner his gun and stepped outside to keep watch.

As he dragged Rashid toward the portable toilet, Rashid begged for mercy in words that sounded like gibberish. Not only were his front teeth shattered, but some of the fragments had cut his tongue. Tanner's baton blow had also caused his lips to swell.

Tanner took Rashid's meaning, understood his fear and dread, but felt neither mercy nor pity for the man. Despite Sara's admonishment that Rashid was politically connected and should be left alive, Tanner would kill him.

The man had been warned what would happen if he sought revenge; now it was time to pay the piper. Besides, the man had threatened Alexa's life. That was unforgivable.

Tanner smashed an elbow into the side of Rashid's head and stunned the man to the brink of unconsciousness. After taking Rashid's wallet and phone, Tanner ripped open the door of the toilet and looked inside.

The stench was horrendous. The bowl was filled to the brim with rancid feces and urine. There were also traces of pale yellow vomit, which contained white chunks. Tanner understood that Rashid had transported the very toilet that Tanner had used on the man in Boston days earlier, and into which Rashid had vomited a lobster dinner.

So much the better, Tanner thought, and he eased Rashid into the toilet head first.

That revived the man, but not in time to save him, and Tanner held Rashid by the legs until the bastard drowned in the feces and liquid filth.

It took well over a minute, and Tanner wondered if Rashid, who was germophobic, had died from lack of air or pure revulsion.

He left the body with its head still inside the bowl and went about collecting everyone's phone, along with the woman's purse and the men's wallets. They would all find their way into the Thames River.

Before leaving, Tanner bashed in the skull of the surviving man, who had been one of the men who had transported the toilet. With luck, the death of everyone involved would eliminate any connection to either himself or Alexa.

After joining Alexa outside, Tanner went for a brisk walk in the night air, hoping that the breeze would wash the smell of that shit box from his clothes.

It didn't, and after returning to his hotel, he sent the garments down a trash chute along with his boots, before taking a long, hot, and very soapy shower.

And still, he could smell the shit.

26

IT'S JUST A MATTER OF TIME

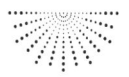

Tanner, shirtless, barefooted, and wearing a pair of jeans, answered a knock on his hotel room door and found Sara looking at him with a worried gaze.

"Omar Ali Rashid is in London," Sara said, and looked down toward the hand Tanner was keeping hidden from sight, a hand no doubt holding a gun.

"Come in, Blake," Tanner said. "And lock that door behind you."

Sara entered, and could hear the shower running from deeper in the suite. When Tanner walked over and laid the gun on the coffee table, Sara relaxed.

"I've been unable to get in contact with you or Alexa, why?"

"Until less than an hour ago, Rashid and his people were keeping Alexa and me too busy to talk. After we handled them, I didn't want to talk with you until I could do so in person."

"And why is that? Did you think I might have been behind Rashid's appearance here?"

"It crossed my mind, but I doubted it was true. Do you know how he found me?"

"Mr. Burke called me tonight and said that it was Brad Grant's doing… independent of Sloane Lennox."

"Independent? I thought he was the man's lapdog?"

"True, but it was Lennox that brought Brad's guilt to Mr. Burke's attention."

"And I would be willing to bet that he did so only after Alexa and I had been in Rashid's hands."

Sara considered that as she nibbled at her bottom lip. "What time did Rashid's people attack you?"

"They grabbed Alexa first, to use as bait, that was around ten o'clock."

"Hmm, given the time difference between here and Connecticut, yes, the two events might have been coordinated, but there's still no proof against Lennox, only Grant."

"Then I'll only kill Grant when we get back," Tanner said, as the sound of the shower water ceased.

Sara nodded toward the bedroom and the bathroom beyond. "Is Alexa all right?"

"Yes, and she killed the woman Rashid had helping him. Rashid and his people made the mistake of thinking she was defenseless."

"And you killed Rashid?"

"With pleasure, as well as everyone he involved. Counting Rashid, there are five dead."

Sara shook her head slightly in wonder. "You are the deadliest man I know."

"It comes in handy, given my profession, but how did your meeting with McManus go?"

Sara was about to answer when Alexa walked out of the bedroom wearing a pair of red silk pajamas. She stared at Sara, then at Tanner, and saw that there was no tension between the two of them.

"Did you tell her about Rashid?"

"Yes, and she tried to warn us."

"How did Rashid know where to find Tanner, Sara?"

Sara explained about Brad Grant and heard Alexa curse in Spanish. After grabbing a bottle of juice from the mini fridge, Alexa sat beside Tanner, and Sara told them about Cole McManus.

"A drunk?" Tanner said.

Sara shook her head. "No, but he does seem headed in that direction. I only told you about the drinking because I want you to know as much as you can. It may help tomorrow."

"Yes, but can he be trusted?" Tanner said.

"I don't see why not. If he betrayed us, Adams would have him killed as well. My biggest concern is whether Adams will even be on that yacht tomorrow. We may be chasing another of his doubles, or he may travel by using some other mode of transportation, or even stay put wherever he is."

"It's all we have right now, so we'll go with it. What time will the yacht be leaving the dock?"

"There's no way to know, but Cole believes it'll be headed toward the US."

Alexa leaned into Tanner, resting her head on his shoulder, as she spoke to Sara.

"Is the yacht under surveillance?"

"Yes, by Burke's security people here, but it's a very loose watch, so that Adams doesn't catch on. They may miss his arrival, but if the yacht leaves in the middle of the night we'll be alerted."

"Whenever it leaves, we follow it," Tanner said. "Then,

I'll use the Seabob to reach it once McManus sends up a signal."

"About that, I spoke to Deke on the way over here and he told me about the changes you wanted to make to the Seabob, are you sure it will be safe?"

"Yes, but it's just a precaution."

"Against betrayal by Cole?"

"Or a leak somewhere else."

"And if I hadn't talked to Deke, would you have told me about the changes?"

"Yes, Blake. If I didn't trust you at all, I wouldn't be here."

Alexa yawned. "To show how much I trust you, I'm going to leave you alone with Tanner while I go off to bed."

Sara stood. "I think we're done, and I could use some sleep myself. I just stopped by to make sure that you were both okay."

Tanner picked up his gun and walked Sara to the door.

"Get some sleep, Blake. I think tomorrow will be a big day."

"And with any luck, it will also be Julien Adams' last day."

Tanner smiled. "It's just a matter of time."

27
IT'S A GO!

The following morning dawned clear and unseasonably warm.

Tanner was still wearing an insulated wet suit, because despite the sunny weather, the water temperature in the Atlantic Ocean was cold. Tanner had no way of knowing how long he might have to be in the water, or even if he was going in at all.

Adams' yacht, the Sea Beast, left London early and set a course for Virginia in the USA. Tanner, Sara, Alexa, and Deke, followed at a distance in a sleek racing boat.

They would stay on the trail of the yacht, and just out of sight, until it dropped anchor, then they would await McManus's signal.

Tanner wore the wet suit, although due to the warmth of the day, he had it unfastened to the waist. As soon as they saw the smoke signal, he would take to the water with the Seabob.

He would don the bulletproof vest as well and ferry the C-4 explosives over to the yacht. Deke assured Tanner that the blast would sink the yacht.

Once they left the explosives behind, Tanner and McManus would have only minutes to get clear of the area around the yacht.

∼

THE SPEEDBOAT WAS MUCH SMALLER THAN THE SAILBOAT they had used while in Greece, and with the temperature being up, Sara, Alexa, and Deke were all dressed in swimwear. Deke had loaded extra fuel aboard the boat. They would need it if they wanted to stay with the yacht, which had huge fuel tanks and dual engines.

Candace had supplied them with coffee in two thermoses along with a stack of sandwiches and fresh fruit. She had no real idea what they were all doing in London, only that they were there for Mr. Burke, and so they were treated as VIP's. Especially Deke, who had gone out twice with Candace.

∼

IN THE LATE AFTERNOON, THE YACHT DROPPED ANCHOR. Deke stopped the boat and drifted, as Tanner lifted a pair of binoculars and looked over at the yacht on the horizon.

As they waited to see what would happen, Alexa held up a sandwich and teased Deke.

"Your girlfriend makes a good sandwich."

"They're from a pub. I doubt Candace can boil water, but she has other talents."

"You're going to miss her when we leave here."

"I might at that, and her accent drives me crazy."

Alexa attempted a British accent and was so bad at it that she began laughing after only uttering a few words.

Deke laughed along, as did Sara, but Tanner was

focused on the yacht, which was barely visible in the distance. He looked as though he were trying to will wisps of smoke to rise from it.

Sara settled beside him. She was dressed in a flesh-toned bathing suit.

"Why don't you eat something? I can watch the yacht."

"I got this, Blake."

"You haven't eaten all day, and I'm sure we'll be able to see any smoke if—"

Tanner turned his head and glared at her.

"I said I got this."

Sara looked surprised by his anger and stood, to move away. Tanner called to her.

"Blake… sit back down."

Sara retook her seat beside Tanner, and he sighed.

"I'm used to working alone. All this, help… it takes a little getting used to."

Sara smiled. "But we have been helpful, haven't we, Deke and I?"

"Yes, along with Garber."

"Good, that's why we're here, and can I ask you a personal question?"

"You can ask me anything, it doesn't mean that I'll answer."

"You're getting a million dollars for this hit, but I don't think you really care about the money, am I right?"

"Yes," Tanner said, surprised that Sara understood that the money was a secondary consideration at best.

"You asked for that much because you believe you're worth that much, and that was before you took down Alvarado."

"Yes."

"I agree. You're worth at least a million dollars. At your

level, it's more a matter of the target being worthy of your time."

"You keep flattering me and you'll give me a swelled head."

"I'm only speaking the truth. But that Sicilian hit man, Maurice Scallato, did you know that one million is the minimum that he'll accept for a hit?"

"No, I didn't know that, but where did you learn that?"

"Brad Grant told me, which means that I should take it with a grain of salt. Besides, there are no pictures of any of the Scallatos. They might be a myth; a family of hit men certainly sounds like a myth."

"They're real. I know someone who had dealings with them years ago."

"Who would that be, your mentor, Tanner Six?"

"I see that you're still researching me, or is it a form of stalking?"

"I'm curious about you, and Alexa gave me some background on the Tanners. So, was I right, did Tanner Six have a run-in with the Scallato family?"

Tanner nodded, even as his eyes drifted down to take in Sara's body. The swimsuit wasn't overly revealing, as it was a one-piece, but its flesh toned color gave the illusion that she was naked. Tanner returned his gaze to her eyes and answered her question.

"Yes, it was Tanner Six, he once went after the same target as Maurice's father, but it was a friendly contest."

"I don't have to ask who won, not if Tanner Six was anything like you."

"No more compliments, Blake, or I'll think you're after something."

Sara leaned closer to Tanner and spoke in a voice that bordered on sultry.

"There is one more thing that I'd like you to know."

"And what would that be?"

Sara grinned. "There's smoke rising from the yacht."

Tanner turned his head and saw that she was right, a thin wisp of white smoke was rising into the sky above the yacht. He looked back at Sara, whose eyes were twinkling as she smiled at him.

"Go get that bastard."

Tanner stood and reached for the vest. "It's show time."

28
BLAST IT ALL

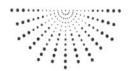

Aboard the yacht, Sea Beast, Cole McManus felt bad about the treachery he was about to commit, but orders were orders and so he would carry them out.

Julien Adams had cut a deal with the CIA just after midnight. Part of the agreement was that he'd be allowed to deal with the threat that Tanner posed.

The agency agreed, and after all, they weren't the ones in the US Government who wanted Adams dead. They had always believed Adams was far more useful as a source of information than an object lesson for other traitors.

In return for that information, Adams would be given a new life in South America, allowed to keep his wealth, and deals would be made inside the Washington corridors of power that would insure no other assassins would be sent after him.

The catalyst for the deal was the fact that Omar Ali Rashid's influential brother was blaming Adams for Rashid's death.

When Adams contacted his bosses, McManus was stunned. Then, he shocked Adams by telling the man that he was a CIA agent, as he was instructed to reveal himself to Adams by his superiors. McManus was also ordered to help Adams in any way he could.

So, he revealed Tanner's assassination plans to Adams and suggested that he fly out of London immediately, before Tanner could get to him.

Adams refused, saying that turning the plan against Tanner would be the perfect way to be rid of him. And so, McManus stood on the deck of the Sea Beast, burning paper in a metal trash basket to lure Tanner to his death.

As the smoke rose into the sky, McManus looked over at Adams and saw that the bastard was smiling.

If I had more balls, I'd grab a gun off one of the bodyguards and shoot the scumbag in the head. McManus thought.

But he wouldn't do it, and when it was all over, he intended to get blind stinking drunk.

∽

ADAMS WATCHED MCMANUS SEND UP THE SIGNAL AS HE SAT in a lounge chair surrounded by eight armed bodyguards.

After Tanner nearly killed him in Greece, Adams called Rashid's home and left a threatening message on the Arab's phone, because Rashid was the only one who could have given his island location away.

Then, when Rashid's body was found by the police the night before, Adams learned from his contacts that Rashid's brother was blaming him for Rashid's death. Surviving one set of assassins was difficult enough. If Rashid's brother was also sending men to kill him, then Adams knew he wouldn't last out the month.

Besides that, the two close calls he suffered in Greece put fear in his heart. He had stared into Tanner's eyes and saw pure death looking back at him. Had he not been in disguise and without one of his doubles, he would be dead, dead and buried.

The CIA was always hungry for information about the players in the Middle-East terrorist community, and Adams would gladly tell them all he knew for a fresh start. He even agreed to set up a CIA trap for some of them to walk into, and from which the CIA could gather more information.

When the CIA told him that they already had a mole in his organization, Adams knew he had made the right choice. His enemies had been drawing near. It was time to cash in his chips and find a new game to play. He could always make deals behind the scenes and increase his wealth in other ways.

Adams smiled. Cyber warfare was a growing field that offered advancement in both wealth and power, perhaps it was time to become a player in that arena.

He signaled to McManus to put out the fire, then watched as the flames were extinguished with seawater. Tanner must have seen the smoke by now and would be on his way to them. Adams rose to get into position and sent McManus a nod.

McManus walked over to the starboard side and back toward the stern, where he tossed a knotted rope overboard.

Adams turned and walked down into the cabin where music played, and where he would be out of sight and the line of fire. Four of the bodyguards followed him while the others hid in strategic spots on the deck. Adams grinned. He couldn't wait to see the look on Tanner's face.

The look on Tanner's face was one of determination, as he held on to the Seabob and aimed it toward Adams' yacht. The C-4 could get wet and still work, but he had the detonators secured against his waist and inside a waterproof pouch.

Deke had rigged a small inflatable ring onto the Seabob that would keep the machine afloat once the ring filled with air. At Tanner's request, Deke had made other alterations to the Seabob, but Tanner hoped he wouldn't need to use them.

He stayed below the surface while traveling the last two hundred yards and was glad to see the end of a knotted rope dangling near the stern, just beneath the water's surface. Even with the sound of the water slapping against the hull, he could hear voices and music drifting from the cabin.

He had just finished rigging the Seabob with the added precautions he and Deke had made and was reaching for the rope when a face peeked over the railing at him.

It was McManus, who matched Sara's description well, and he looked nervous, as he called down to him in a loud hoarse whisper.

"Tanner, get your ass up here before someone sees us."

Tanner gazed over at the Seabob and saw that it was staying put against the side of the yacht. Along with the inflatable ring, Deke had added a patch with a strong adhesive to a section of the Seabob's outer casing. That small section was an add-on and not an original part of the machine. When it came time to leave, Tanner could detach the Seabob from it with ease and take off.

But until he returned to the water, the Seabob would stay in place. If all went well, Tanner and McManus would be going back over the side and using the craft to leave the area before the bomb detonated.

Tanner climbed up the rope. He had to mostly use his arms, as the side of the boat was slick from the sea spray.

His broken right pinkie finger was more annoying than painful, but it didn't interfere enough to affect his grip on the rope, and after reaching the rail, McManus helped him over the side by grabbing his hands and tugging.

When McManus kept gripping his hands, Tanner stared at him, and McManus held on to him while whispering the words, "I'm sorry, man."

Two armed guards appeared, then two more, and McManus released Tanner and moved away fast.

"Get back from the rail motherfucker or we'll blow your ass into tomorrow," one of the men said.

Tanner put his hands in the air and remained silent. The man told him to walk toward him. Tanner followed orders, but when the man told him to sit in front of the railing near the cabin door, Tanner, with his hands still raised up high, walked over to the port side of the yacht before sitting down.

The man rushed over and kicked him on the leg.

"When I tell you to sit, I mean sit, not walk. Now, very slowly hand over the detonators."

Tanner complied and removed the pouch, as he did so, he took a look at his watch and saw that there was just over two minutes left.

The man then instructed him to take off the vest and to slide it over toward McManus, who had reappeared and was standing to Tanner's left holding a pair of handcuffs.

The handcuffs would be a problem, but not an insurmountable one, since Tanner saw McManus place the key to the cuffs in his right front pocket. McManus cuffed Tanner's left wrist to the brass railing at his back, and Tanner asked him a question.

"Is Blake a part of this?"

"Sara? No, and she'll want my balls for souvenirs once she's learned what's happened."

"Where's Adams?" Tanner said. "The real Adams."

"I'm here," a voice said, and Julien Adams walked out of the ship's cabin and glared down at Tanner.

Tanner stared back at him and asked a question. "You're a tough man to kill Adams, but how do I know you're not another double?"

Adams grinned, grabbed his bottom lip, and pulled it down so that Tanner could see there was no tattoo there. Tanner took another glance at his watch and saw that there was less than a minute left.

"I'm the genuine article. The man you killed in Greece was one of three doubles. I sent the last one to Dubai, where he'll likely be slain by an angry Arab who believes I had his brother killed."

"How much did it cost to get McManus here to sell out?"

"Oh, you misunderstand, McManus is just doing his job. The CIA and I have come to terms, and you, Tanner, you were part of the deal."

McManus was checking out the vest while Adams talked, and he became confused by what he found.

"The packets in this vest aren't C-4, they're just common modeling clay."

A check of the watch revealed that there were only twelve seconds left.

McManus moved directly in front of Tanner and held the vest up.

"What the hell is this?"

Tanner bucked his hips up off the deck and locked his legs around McManus's waist.

A guard shouted, McManus struggled to break free, and the C-4 attached to the Seabob exploded. The blast rocked the yacht while blowing a hole in its side that you could drive a car through, which caused the vessel to lean sharply starboard.

The line of guards all stumbled backwards into the rail, with more than one of them firing rounds into the air as they lost their balance. Most of the men fell over the rail and into the water below, but one man managed to hold on, while dangling over the side.

Adams had fallen to his knees, and then slid on his stomach into the side of the cabin wall, thudding his head into it. The yacht canted increasingly toward starboard while sinking lower into the sea.

Tanner's hold on McManus was slipping loose, but not before he tore at his pocket and freed the key to the handcuffs. With the key in his possession, Tanner released McManus. The CIA agent had been leaning rearward in an effort to break Tanner's grasp on his waist, and once released, he went tumbling backwards at a great speed.

McManus's left arm slammed into the last of the guards, who had just managed to climb back up. The two of them went tumbling over the side while shouting in fright.

Tanner freed his wrist from the cuffs and smiled over at Adams, who had made it to his feet and had leaned against the outside cabin wall.

"Alone at last," Tanner said.

Adams let out a shriek of fright and stumbled over to the cabin door, as he hoped to escape his fate.

That was when the second blast occurred.

A spare propane tank that was slated to be used for cooking in the galley was damaged by the first explosion. The resulting gas leak encountered flames and exploded. The sound of the blast was followed by screams coming from the cabin.

Adams fell again, as a man who was aflame and dressed as a cook rushed onto the deck and dived over the side. And while the seawater did extinguish his flaming clothing, the man inadvertently set the surface of the water on fire, as there was a slick of oil floating on it, oil mixed with fuel.

Adams' guards, along with McManus, had their faces seared by the flames, and their cries carried up from the water.

Tanner reached out and grabbed Adams' by the hair, to drag him closer. He then cuffed Adams' wrist to the rail, as McManus had recently done to him.

Yet a third explosion went off, and from deep within the ship, where several tanks were stored for scuba diving. The blast tore a second hole in the hull and was so powerful that it blew the cabin door open and left it hanging by a single hinge.

Tanner lost his balance but managed to grab onto Adams and pull himself up, only to find that he was standing at a steep angle and forced to grab hold of the railing.

The screams of the men in the water intensified, while also sounding hoarse, and guttural.

Then, a great plume of black smoke poured out of the open cabin door, and beyond, down in the seating area of the saloon, there were flames visible.

Tanner looked out at the water and realized that the yacht was going down fast. He showed Adams the handcuff key. The man snatched out a hand for it with eyes wide from panic and a chest heaving in fear. Tanner tossed the handcuff key over the side and Adams whimpered and moaned.

"You deserve to drown, Adams. You deserve every ounce of the terror you're feeling, but I have a job to do."

Tanner stunned Adams with a knee to the chin, before dropping down behind him and wrapping his arms around the man's neck, which he broke with a savage twist, leaving Adams' head to hang loosely.

The angle of the sinking yacht increased, and Tanner found it a struggle just to stand.

The port side of the boat was free of bodies, but there were flames burning atop the water, fed by a mixture of oil and fuel.

Tanner shielded his face as well as he could with his arms and hoped that the wet suit he wore would protect his body. Then he dove into the flames and sank beneath the surface.

Adams was dead, truly dead, and the hit was done.

29

MISSION ACCOMPLISHED

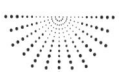

When the C-4 went off, Sara, Deke, and Alexa knew that something had gone wrong, because of the timing.

Tanner was to initially set the detonator on the C-4 to activate the explosive after only a few minutes. However, if things had gone as planned, Tanner would have reset the detonator, detached the Seabob from the container holding the C-4, and given himself and McManus more time to gain distance from the yacht.

Sara forced herself to look away from the growing cloud of smoke in the distance and took charge. "I'll take the wheel, Deke. You scan ahead by using the scope on your rifle. If you spot a threat, kill it."

When Sara looked back at Alexa, she saw the worried look on her face. Sara called to her, but had to call again, as Alexa seemed lost in thought.

When Alexa finally turned and looked at her, Sara smiled. "He's fine. He's a Tanner, right?"

Alexa nodded and sent a weak smile back at Sara.

Sara pointed to her bag, which was tucked under a

seat. "Take out the binoculars and search the water. It looks like Tanner will need to be picked up."

~

Their boat's speed got them to the area in short order, but not before a second, and then a third and final explosion went off. Sara slowed their approach at that point and they could see that the yacht was listing to starboard and on fire.

Deke spotted the bodies floating in the water first, and Alexa trained the binoculars on each one, while praying that Tanner would not be among them.

"They look burned," Alexa said.

Because of the current, the bodies were floating in their direction, and possibly being pushed along by the waves of heat the huge fire burning on the water produced. In the center of the flames, only the upper section of the yacht's mast remained above the water, it was jutting out at a steep angle and turning black from the smoke.

Sara slowed the boat even more to navigate around the blaze, while also trying to avoid the smoke being blown toward them by the sea breeze. As she moved closer, she caught sight of the floating corpse of Cole McManus.

McManus' face was charred on one side while his hair was singed. His mouth was locked in a rictus of pain, but other than the burns on his neck and face, Sara saw that the rest of his body had been spared the flames. Understanding came to her then, and she knew that McManus' likely cause of death was from inhaling the superheated fumes of the fire, when one of the explosions occurred.

Sara was circumnavigating the flames when Deke spotted movement to their right, about fifty yards away.

It was Tanner.

Alexa laughed with relief, as did Sara, while Deke readied a line with an attached life preserver and tossed it to Tanner.

Tanner had suffered a minor burn on his left cheek while diving through the flames but was otherwise all right. He responded to Alexa's kiss before speaking to Sara.

"McManus had orders to turn me over to Adams. His heart wasn't in it though, and he actually apologized as he did it."

"Cole made his choice and it cost him, but how are you, Tanner?"

"I'm good, Blake, and Adams is dead. They'll find his body handcuffed to a piece of the ship's railing."

Sara smiled and grabbed a satellite phone. "Deke, please take us back in. While you're doing that, I've a call to make to Mr. Burke."

"You got it, Sara," Deke said. He headed the boat back toward London, as above them, the sky began to darken toward night.

THE FOLLOWING MORNING, THEY WERE ALL GATHERED IN the conference room at Burke UK and staring at a video image of Conrad Burke over a secured connection.

"The body has been recovered and verified to be the real Julien Adams. Good work, Tanner, and congratulations, Miss Blake."

"Thank you, sir," Sara said. "And I'll be back by this evening. We're headed to the airport after this meeting."

"I'd like to see you here as well, Tanner," Burke said. "I

want to discuss what Brad Grant did. I assure you that Sloane Lennox had no part in that. I know Sloane well, and yes, the man can be an ass at times, but he would never be behind a stunt like that."

"That 'stunt' could have gotten Alexa killed, Burke, but I'll give Lennox the benefit of the doubt. Brad Grant won't be so lucky."

"I hear you. And I hope you'll keep working with us. The government was pleased with the results."

"Is there more work?"

"I believe so, my contact said that he'll get back to me with the details, but from what he said, it sounds domestic, and will keep you in the states."

"I'm willing," Tanner said, "But I want to renegotiate our terms."

Burke sighed. "How much more do you want?"

Tanner shook his head. "The same million I was paid last time, but I want Deke here on call, and he'll get five percent of that million, on top of whatever you're paying him, also, send a one-time payment of fifty grand Garber's way. If he hadn't trained me to use the Seabob, this hit would have never happened."

Deke placed a hand on Tanner's shoulder. "That's damn generous, Tanner, but I was just doing my job, man."

"You deserve it, Deke."

"What about Miss Blake, Tanner?" Burke asked.

Tanner turned his head and looked at Sara. "I'm sure you pay her well already, Burke."

Sara smiled. "I'm adequately compensated, yes."

"I'll see that the money is handled when the next contract comes in," Burke said. "Oh, and Miss Blake, expect a raise in pay. I also like to reward talent."

"Thank you, sir."

"Have a good flight home, people," Burke said, and ended the call.

∽

Before climbing into the limo that would take them to the airport, the group said goodbye to the vivacious Candace Oliver. Deke's farewell took longer, as he and Candace shared several kisses among whispers.

Sara smirked as Deke settled beside her in the rear of the limo. "I'm glad that one of us enjoyed themselves while we were in London."

"Yeah, Candace was fun to be around," Deke said, "and I'll miss her."

An hour later, they were on the Burke corporate jet and headed home.

Mission accomplished.

30

AN OFFER TO STAY

A few days later, Sara was back in Connecticut and rummaging through a storage unit. She was loading up her car with things she would take to her new apartment.

She would be taking the unit in Deke's building and stop living out of a hotel room. It was one more step toward building a new life. Although she wasn't happy, she was feeling more contented and settled.

As she stooped to grab a box of DVD's from the bottom of a bookcase, Sara heard someone enter the unit behind her and slam down the metal door. The storage unit was a ten-foot square cube of space that had thin steel walls and a concrete floor.

It was mid-morning on a weekday and the nearest person around was the clerk in the office, which was located far from Sara's unit.

Sara collapsed onto the floor in pain, as a stun gun was pressed against her neck. When she rolled onto her back, she squinted at the light in the ceiling, then realized that Brad Grant was standing over her. Sara found herself helpless to stop Grant as he proceeded to bind her wrists together.

~

By the time Sara recovered from the Taser blast, her hands were bound behind her back and there was a strip of tape covering her mouth. Grant had propped her up in a corner and was sitting before her in a folding chair. Brad Grant hadn't shaved in days and had the beginnings of a beard, while his hair had been cut very short.

He smiled down at Sara. "I hear through the grapevine that Tanner killed Adams, the lucky bastard."

Sara spoke, but her words came out muffled behind the tape.

Grant took out a gun from his jacket pocket and pointed it at Sara. "I'll remove the tape, but if you scream, I'll shoot you."

Sara nodded her understanding, and Grant ripped off the tape, but only after his eyes roamed over her body.

After taking a moment to moisten her dry lips, Sara asked a question. "Did you contact Omar Ali Rashid on Sloane Lennox's orders?"

"Lennox didn't know shit about it. I did it on my own to open up a slot for Maurice Scallato. It was Scallato's idea to contact Rashid."

"You communicate with Scallato?"

"Yeah, but only over the internet. I've been trying to get him here ever since I found out that Burke was starting a wet works division for the government. The man would have been perfect, but instead, you forced Tanner on us."

"Tanner is better than Scallato," Sara said.

"How do you know that?"

"Tanner is better than anyone."

Grant laughed. "I knew it. You're fucking Tanner, aren't you? You'll fuck that piece of shit but won't give me the time of day? What a cunt."

Sara tried to free her hands but found it useless. She decided to keep Grant talking if she could. If he was talking, he wouldn't be doing other things, and she had caught the gleam of lust in his eyes as he looked her over.

"What exactly did Scallato advise you to do, Brad?"

"I told him what was going on and he asked me to contact Rashid and give him Tanner's whereabouts. He said if Tanner was as good as he thinks he is, then he shouldn't have a problem handling Rashid."

"How do you contact him? What email address is he using?" Sara asked.

Grant hadn't heard her; he was occupied with looking her over again. Sara was dressed in an old pair of jeans and a white sweatshirt.

The shirt had ridden up to reveal her midsection, which was taut and tanned. Having Sara bound and helpless was giving Grant bad ideas. He roughly plastered the piece of tape back over her mouth and then moved his hands under her sweatshirt to fondle her breasts through the fabric of her bra. When she kicked out at him and just barely missed his crotch, Grant punched her hard twice on the chin, and Sara had to fight to stay conscious.

Grant was yanking down Sara's jeans when the door behind him slid up and a voice shouted a command.

"Police, put your hands in the air!"

Grant foolishly reached down for his gun and the cop and his partner fired their weapons, striking him six times.

Grant moaned and fell onto Sara. She watched the light fade from his eyes, as his blood soaked into her shirt.

Hours later, Tanner grimaced as he looked at the bruise on Sara's chin. By the slow, deliberate way she spoke, he could tell that her jaw ached.

"The son of a bitch tried to rape you?"

"Yes, and he might have if the clerk in the office hadn't been watching the surveillance cameras when Brad entered my storage unit. He'd been holding only a stun gun at the time, but the clerk thought it was pistol and she called the cops."

They were inside Sara's apartment, which was filled with cartons from her storage unit. She didn't have a bed, but the delivery truck was due at any time. She had asked Tanner to meet with her there, since she couldn't leave the apartment and miss getting her delivery.

When she told Tanner that Grant said that Maurice Scallato was behind Rashid's appearance in London, the hit man surprised her by smiling.

"It sounds like someone doesn't like competition," Tanner said.

"This could be serious, Tanner. Do you think Scallato has targeted you?"

"No, I think he saw an opportunity to get me out of the way without dirtying his hands and he took it. If I'm not around, Burke might use him to fulfill contracts. Like I said, he probably looks on me as competition."

"Is he really as good as you are?" Sara asked.

"We're in the same league, there's no doubt about that. If the rumors are true, Scallato is the man who did the hit on that Saudi prince last month. That was a nice piece of work, given that the man was being guarded inside an underground bunker at the time. Scallato sneaked by all the security measures, killed the prince, and escaped without once being seen. Masterful, and it's no wonder that his nickname is 'The Ghost.'"

"You admire him, then?"

"I admire his work."

"If he does view you as a threat, you may have to kill him someday."

"Yes."

"I'm going to research Scallato."

"Why?"

"As a precaution, the more we know about him, the better prepared we'll be in case he makes another move against you."

"I have no objections, but I doubt you'll find anything," Tanner said.

They then grew silent as they stared at each other. The silence wasn't awkward or uncomfortable, nor was it the easy silence that occurs between two friends. It was simply silence, and neither Tanner nor Sara felt the need to end it.

When the buzzer on the wall sounded off, Sara broke eye contact and walked over to the intercom beside the door.

"Yes, who is it?"

"We're delivering your new bed," A young male voice told her, and Sara hit a button that would unlock the door downstairs.

Tanner gestured at the cartons scattered around. "A new start, hmm?"

"Yes, at least I hope so."

They stared at each other again, until Tanner sent her a nod and walked toward the door to leave.

"I'll see you around, Blake." He stepped out of the apartment, and in the hallway, the elevator doors opened, and two burly men walked off and began leaning the sections of Sara's new bed against a wall.

Tanner watched the men until they carried a metal bedframe into the apartment.

"Would you like me to stay until after they set up the bed?"

Sara's mouth parted in surprise and her eyes narrowed. "Why Tanner, are you offering to help me break in the mattress?"

Tanner let out a sigh. "No, Blake, but after what Grant tried to do to you earlier… I thought you might be a little wary of being alone with two strange men."

Sara walked over and gently placed her hand on his arm. "I'm sorry. That was very thoughtful of you to offer to stay, but no, I'll be all right. I'm tougher than I look."

"Don't I know it," Tanner said.

He let her hand slip away and stepped aboard the elevator. The two of them stared at each other once again, until the elevator closed and carried him away.

TANNER RETURNS

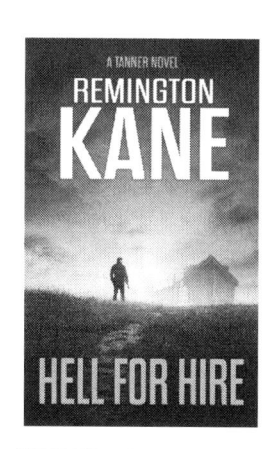

HELL FOR HIRE - BOOK 13

AFTERWORD

Thank you,

REMINGTON KANE

JOIN MY INNER CIRCLE

You'll receive FREE books, such as,

SLAY BELLS – A TANNER NOVEL – BOOK 0
TAKEN! ALPHABET SERIES – 26 ORIGINAL TAKEN! TALES

Also – Exclusive short stories featuring TANNER, along with other books.

TO BECOME AN INNER CIRCLE MEMBER, GO TO:
http://remingtonkane.com/mailing-list/

ALSO BY REMINGTON KANE

The TANNER Series in order

INEVITABLE I - A Tanner Novel - Book 1

KILL IN PLAIN SIGHT - A Tanner Novel - Book 2

MAKING A KILLING ON WALL STREET - A Tanner Novel - Book 3

THE FIRST ONE TO DIE LOSES - A Tanner Novel - Book 4

THE LIFE & DEATH OF CODY PARKER - A Tanner Novel - Book 5

WAR - A Tanner Novel- A Tanner Novel - Book 6

SUICIDE OR DEATH - A Tanner Novel - Book 7

TWO FOR THE KILL - A Tanner Novel - Book 8

BALLET OF DEATH - A Tanner Novel - Book 9

MORE DANGEROUS THAN MAN - A Tanner Novel - Book 10

TANNER TIMES TWO - A Tanner Novel - Book 11

OCCUPATION: DEATH - A Tanner Novel - Book 12

HELL FOR HIRE - A Tanner Novel - Book 13

A HOME TO DIE FOR - A Tanner Novel - Book 14

FIRE WITH FIRE - A Tanner Novel - Book 15

TO KILL A KILLER - A Tanner Novel - Book 16

WHITE HELL – A Tanner Novel - Book 17

MANHATTAN HIT MAN – A Tanner Novel - Book 18

ONE HUNDRED YEARS OF TANNER – A Tanner Novel -

Book 19

REVELATIONS - A Tanner Novel - Book 20

THE SPY GAME - A Tanner Novel - Book 21

A VICTIM OF CIRCUMSTANCE - A Tanner Novel - Book 22

A MAN OF RESPECT - A Tanner Novel - Book 23

THE MAN, THE MYTH - A Tanner Novel - Book 24

ALL-OUT WAR - A Tanner Novel - Book 25

THE REAL DEAL - A Tanner Novel - Book 26

WAR ZONE - A Tanner Novel - Book 27

ULTIMATE ASSASSIN - A Tanner Novel - Book 28

KNIGHT TIME - A Tanner Novel - Book 29

PROTECTOR - A Tanner Novel - Book 30

BULLETS BEFORE BREAKFAST - A Tanner Novel - Book 31

VENGEANCE - A Tanner Novel - Book 32

TARGET: TANNER - A Tanner Novel - Book 33

BLACK SHEEP - A Tanner Novel - Book 34

FLESH AND BLOOD - A Tanner Novel - Book 35

NEVER SEE IT COMING - A Tanner Novel - Book 36

MISSING - A Tanner Novel - Book 37

CONTENDER - A Tanner Novel - Book 38

TO SERVE AND PROTECT - A Tanner Novel - Book 39

STALKING HORSE - A Tanner Novel - Book 40

THE EVIL OF TWO LESSERS - A Tanner Novel - Book 41

SINS OF THE FATHER AND MOTHER - A Tanner Novel - Book 42

SOULLESS - A Tanner Novel - Book 43

BLUE STEELE - DADDY'S GIRL - Book 7 & the Series Finale

The CALIBER DETECTIVE AGENCY Series in order

CALIBER DETECTIVE AGENCY - GENERATIONS- Book 1

CALIBER DETECTIVE AGENCY - TEMPTATION- Book 2

CALIBER DETECTIVE AGENCY - A RANSOM PAID IN BLOOD- Book 3

CALIBER DETECTIVE AGENCY - MISSING- Book 4

CALIBER DETECTIVE AGENCY - DECEPTION- Book 5

CALIBER DETECTIVE AGENCY - CRUCIBLE- Book 6

CALIBER DETECTIVE AGENCY – LEGENDARY – Book 7

CALIBER DETECTIVE AGENCY – WE ARE GATHERED HERE TODAY - Book 8

CALIBER DETECTIVE AGENCY - MEANS, MOTIVE, and OPPORTUNITY - Book 9 & the Series Finale

THE TAKEN!/TANNER Series in order

THE CONTRACT: KILL JESSICA WHITE - Taken!/Tanner - Book 1

UNFINISHED BUSINESS – Taken!/Tanner – Book 2

THE ABDUCTION OF THOMAS LAWSON - Taken!/Tanner – Book 3

PREDATOR - Taken!/Tanner - Book 4

DETECTIVE PIERCE Series in order

MONSTERS - A Detective Pierce Novel - Book 1

DEMONS - A Detective Pierce Novel - Book 2

ANGELS - A Detective Pierce Novel - Book 3

THE OCEAN BEACH ISLAND Series in order

THE MANY AND THE ONE - Book 1

SINS & SECOND CHANES - Book 2

DRY ADULTERY, WET AMBITION - Book 3

OF TONGUE AND PEN - Book 4

ALL GOOD THINGS… - Book 5

LITTLE WHITE SINS - Book 6

THE LIGHT OF DARKNESS - Book 7

STERN ISLAND - Book 8 & the Series Finale

THE REVENGE Series in order

JOHNNY REVENGE - The Revenge Series - Book 1

THE APPOINTMENT KILLER - The Revenge Series - Book 2

AN I FOR AN I - The Revenge Series - Book 3

ALSO

THE EFFECT: Reality is changing!

THE FIX-IT MAN: A Tale of True Love and Revenge

DOUBLE OR NOTHING

PARKER & KNIGHT

REDEMPTION: Someone's taken her

DESOLATION LAKE

TIME TRAVEL TALES & OTHER SHORT STORIES

OCCUPATION: DEATH
Copyright © REMINGTON KANE, 2016
YEAR ZERO PUBLISHING

This book is a work of fiction. Names, characters, places and incidents either are products of the author's imagination or are used fictitiously.

Any resemblance to actual events or locales or persons, living or dead, is entirely coincidental.

All rights reserved. Except as permitted under the U.S. Copyright Act of 1976, no part of this publication may be reproduced, distributed or transmitted in any form or by any means, or stored in a database or retrieval system, without the prior written permission of the publisher.

❋ Created with Vellum

Printed in Great Britain
by Amazon